WHO WILL RESCUE US?

A LOVE STORY

"The plot—intriguing. The subject—heart-wrenching. The story—must be told. *Who Will Rescue Us?: A Love Story* is a touching story that will grab your heart and not let go. A well-done, must-read."

—CINDY K. SPROLES

Best-selling author of *This Is Where It Ends*

"*Who Will Rescue Us?: A Love Story* is a timely must-read by award-winning author Judy DuCharme. There is nothing more valuable than our children, and this novella tackles the issue of trafficking head on. It also blends in a love story about a couple who fall in love and retrieve children who have been left behind by a family member. The kids learn and adapt, and some even find how powerful the gift of forgiveness can be. Grab this wonderful and moving piece of work by Judy."

—DEL DUDUIT

Author and agent

"Judy DuCharme's new novella, *Who Will Rescue Us?: A Love Story*, explores the trauma of a Sofia, a young mother from Bolivia who nearly drowns as she crosses the Rio Grande River trying to illegally enter the United States. The story explores the frightening aspects of being a new immigrant and then confronts the terror of another part of America's underbelly—child trafficking. For all the trauma and dramatic tragedy found in its pages, however, the central theme of the novella is about love.

As with all of DuCharme's books, *Who Will Rescue Us?: A Love Story* contains a Christian message about acceptance, love, healing, forgiveness, and eventual redemption. The message is wrapped into a story that keeps the reader turning the pages, however; and in the end, this particular novella becomes a celebration of what ought to be in this troubled world of ours."

—THOMAS DAVIS

Acclaimed author

In the Unsettled Homeland of Dreams and *Prophecy of the Wolf*

"As a Christian psychotherapist in private practice for over twenty-five years, I have had the humbling privilege of working with many who have been trafficked and who have managed to escape. The unspeakable horrors and trauma these individuals have gone through is beyond comprehension and utterly heartbreaking.

In Judy DuCharme's book, *Who Will Rescue Us?: A Love Story,* she portrays a very realistic glimpse into the world of child sex trafficking. She carefully approaches this extremely difficult issue with tender care and also sends out a call to action to help the victims of this abhorrent crime. Even though this book is technically a work of fiction, it accurately represents the reality of what the victims endure at the hands of their abductors. Although the journey to healing for the victims is by no means a short or easy one, when God is a part of that healing journey, they can be set free and move forward as they learn to process their trauma and allow God to heal the shattered pieces of their hearts.

This is a read that is not only compelling, skillfully rendered, and informative but also very necessary in the day and age in which we live."

—SUSAN C. BROZEK, M.S.W., L.C.S.W.

Director/Founder, and Licensed Clinical Psychotherapist

at Healing Word Psychotherapy Services, LLC

#1 Bestselling Author

International Radio Broadcast Host of "The Way of Healing" at

Reaching Out Radio

"This story humanizes the statistics. The assault of the news cycle can numb us to the human suffering behind immigration. *Who Will Rescue Us?: A Love Story* challenges the heart to care and really see each precious person."

—KIRSTEN PANACHYDA
Speaker and author
Among Lions: Fighting for Faith and Finding Your Rest While Parenting a Child with Mental Illness

"Inspired by true events, Judy DuCharme takes us beyond the headlines to tell a much-needed story of pain, separation, suffering, and hope. She takes us into the dark underbelly of the immigrant experience but does not leave us there. Recommended for all ages."

—LYNNE TAGAWA
Author of *The Shenandoah Road*

"Judy so lovingly tells an impactful story that awakens every emotion about the overwhelming truth of the horrors of child trafficking going on, not just in this country but, sadly, all over the world today. It is filled with lessons on the importance of being cautious and aware of your surroundings, forgiving in order to heal, as well as relying on the depths of God's love that gets you through it. Having been through abuse myself as a young person, I can truly attest to God's faithfulness, mercy, love, and healing. It is of the greatest importance to not only trust in God's faithfulness but also to forgive fully so that you may be set free from the endless pain and sorrow. Believe in His Word when he says He restores and makes new."

—MAXI UNVERFERTH
Blessed by the BEST—so thankful

WHO WILL RESCUE US?

A LOVE STORY

JUDY DUCHARME

AMBASSADOR INTERNATIONAL
GREENVILLE, SOUTH CAROLINA & BELFAST, NORTHERN IRELAND

www.ambassador-international.com

WHO WILL RESCUE US? A LOVE STORY

Paperback ISBN: 978-1-64960-627-3
eISBN: 978-1-64960-676-1

Cover design by Hannah Linder Design
Interior Typesetting by Dentelle Design
Editing by Katie Cruice Smith

Ambassador International titles may be purchased in bulk for education, business, fundraising, or sales promotional use. For information, please email sales@emeraldhouse.com.

AMBASSADOR INTERNATIONAL
Emerald House
411 University Ridge, Suite B14
Greenville, SC 29601
United States
www.ambassador-international.com

AMBASSADOR BOOKS
The Mount
2 Woodstock Link
Belfast, BT6 8DD
Northern Ireland, United Kingdom
www.ambassadormedia.co.uk

The colophon is a trademark of Ambassador, a Christian publishing company.

This story is dedicated to those who shared their story with me, to the many children who have fallen prey to the wicked reality of trafficking, and to the wonderful people who have stepped in to provide rescue.

AUTHOR'S NOTE

This is the story of rescuers and survivors of an evil practice. Some of the non-trafficking stories are true. Although the trafficking and the rescues are fiction, they are the reality seen daily in the news and experienced daily by too many children. I began this novella before I saw the movie *Sound of Freedom*. At the end of the movie, the star, Jim Caviezel, spoke to the audience and stated that the storytellers are the most important people in the world. At that point, I committed to finishing this book. My prayer is that you enjoy it. Yes, enjoy. I believe you'll fall in love with the children and relish the love story, as well as the strategies, of the rescuers. However, become aware, be shocked, and become committed to do your part to stop the heinous practice of trafficking. There are resources at the end of the book. If you see someone you suspect is being trafficked, contact authorities, call the number, and pray for those so deeply harmed in this all-too-common situation in our culture.

I want to express my thanks to those who shared stories, to the makers of *Sound of Freedom*, to those of my Word Weavers critique group who cheered me on and have always helped me improve my writing, and especially to those who assist in rescues and counseling those who have suffered.

Now, behold, I release you today from the chains on your hands.

—Jeremiah 40:4

CHAPTER ONE

MARCH 1981

The moon stood high in the sky—the best time, or so they said. Sofia groaned. The attempt before had been a great failure. She'd crossed easy enough, but she'd been caught and sent back. A shiver tickled her back as the breeze picked up. Did the wind make the current stronger? The iciness in her stomach made her double over. She couldn't swim. She straightened and swallowed. The others looked nervous as well, but they had people with them.

Her sister Camila had crossed beside her the first time. And so had the snakes in the river. Her stomach roiled within, and her teeth clenched involuntarily. She could already hear the frogs.

Sofia whispered, "Alone."

But she would not avail herself of the opportunity to return to the children. Manuel and Isobel were safe with cousins. A tear slid down her cheek. She sent up a silent prayer. *Keep them safe, Lord, until I can return for them.* She shook her head. Would she be able to go back for them soon—once she made it safely . . . assuming she made it safely?

Camila had somehow arrived in Washington, D.C. Hopefully, the money Sofia had would get her there. She'd spent so much on the first flight from Bolivia and now had to do it again. Camila had sent a little, and she'd saved a bit more working as a waitress. Still, four months provided little. The children were with Cousin Marisa; but after illness struck, they were sent to Luisa. She had told Sofia not to return until she could take the children with her and to just send her waitress money for their care. Did she only want money? Fortunately, Sofia had landed the restaurant job and stayed with another friend, but not seeing the kids tore at her heart.

How could she continue even now without her children? How could she bear it? Manuel, only six, had cried when she left. Isobel, two years older, had clung to her but promised to take care of her little brother. Sofia knew she must succeed. She couldn't go back. She must cross. She'd already been away from them too long. Would Luisa love them?

Those around her slid down the bank and entered the water, its blackness lit only by the shiny path the moon's reflection spread across the river. The shallower water of the Rio Grande flowed before her. Sofia stepped in and caught her breath. The coldness penetrated her legs as well as her soul. Her clothes, now saturated, clung to her and added weight to her movement. She lifted her chin and kept walking. She hefted her bag as high as she could. The river rose to her armpits, but they said it would get no deeper. Just stay in the line. Those in front started swimming.

Please, God. I can't swim.

Sofia gulped, and her legs gave out. The current caught her. Sofia flailed. The river water invaded her mouth, and coughing ensued. Her cry for help became a gurgle. No one could help. Fear shouted in her mind.

My babies. God, Dios, take care of them. Help me, please.

A strong hand wrapped around her arm and yanked. A voice commanded, "Climb onto my back, lady!"

Sofia gurgled and shook her head. The grip of the man's hand sent pain up to her shoulder.

He shouted again. "Woman! Climb onto my back. Now!"

Sofia awoke from her stupor and clambered onto the man's back. She grasped his shoulder but could only grip his shirt. She swung a leg over his back but failed to fully land there. She clung to him, his shirt in one hand and her bag in the other. Would his shirt rip and send her into the depths of the Rio Grande?

The man struggled to move forward. After every few steps or strokes, he pushed on her side to keep her from slipping off. Eventually, the screams of fear in her mind quieted, but then she heard the cries of the little ones with their parents, of the wives with their husbands. She let the tears run down her face. Everything was wet, anyway. She prayed the children would make it. She prayed her own children survived. No, thrived. She shouldn't have left them; but since Miguel had divorced her, what was she to do?

The man let go. Sofia plopped in the water and screamed.

The man shushed her. "Be quiet. We're across."

"Thank you. Mucho gracias." She reached toward him. How could she repay?

"De nada. No problem, lady." With that, he disappeared into the blackness of the night.

Sofia waded to shore, one of the last to do so. The families ran into the brush. She saw headlights and trembled. Would she be caught again? Others huddled near the shore.

Sofia hugged herself. She wanted to throw herself to the ground, and . . . what? Sleep? Dry off? Cry? Kiss the ground? This was the United States. She'd made it—once more. She sobbed.

A woman nearby grabbed her hand. "We have people picking us up. We can give you a ride, okay?"

"Are you sure it isn't the police? To capture and send us back?"

"Come. We'll hide till we are sure."

Sofia allowed the woman to lead her into the brush and behind some rocks. The moon cast long shadows, those of bushes swaying with the breeze. She closed her eyes. The specters might not be shrubs but people committed to returning them to the other side. She forced herself to take in the surroundings. Three men and four women crouched along with two little ones. Sofia's breath caught. The little faces so resembled her own children. She wanted to sob, but she smiled and wrapped her arms around them. She knew they needed to be quiet. She could express her thanks by helping them.

She whispered in each ear, "Be quiet, dear ones. It'll be all right."

She heard a whistle, followed by a bird call. At that, the woman grabbed her hand and pulled her to her feet. "Come with us."

Sofia took the children's hands and followed to the station wagon. She scrambled in the back with the woman and her children. No one said a word. The vehicle stank of cigarettes and sweat, but the seats were comfortable, though lumpy. Her eyes drooped with weariness, and she submitted herself to her exhaustion.

Manuel snuggled closer to his sister. The thin blanket offered little warmth, and the air that leaked through the walls chilled him. Isobel was warm. She wrapped her arms around him, and they fell asleep.

The door slammed. The boy opened his eyes.

"What did I tell you? Boys and girls do not sleep together. I'll not have that in my home. Get up! Now!"

Manuel sat up and rubbed his eyes. "But, Tía, it's cold. Isobel is keeping . . ."

Tía Luisa grabbed his arm. "You will not sleep in the same bed. Isobel, get to the kitchen and clean up the dishes. Manuel, get your school clothes on and sweep this floor. If there is any food left from breakfast, you can have it. Be quick, or you'll be late to school. Your cousins are all ready to go."

Isobel stood. She shivered in her little nightgown. "Tía Luisa, why did you not wake us?"

Tía Luisa raised her hand. "Do not talk back to me, young lady. It will earn you a slap next time."

"Yes, Tía." Isobel hung her head and tried to hide the clenching of her hands.

Tía marched from the drafty porch that had become their bedroom, once more slamming the door.

"Hurry, Manny. She's mad; and if we take too much time, we won't get to school. It's warmer there."

"Why is she so mad, Bella?" Manny puckered his lips. It always meant he was close to crying when he wanted to be strong. He shook his head to stop tears, tossing his unruly black hair every which way.

"I don't know."

He wanted Isobel to hug him, but there was no time. He needed a hug—they both did—but thinking it would only bring angry tears. And hugs would never happen with Tía Luisa.

"When will Mama come back? I miss her." His large brown eyes penetrated hers.

"Manny, I don't know that either. I hope soon. But now, hurry. We have work to do before school starts."

CHAPTER TWO

Sofia stirred. How long had she slept? A bit of dried drool stuck to her cheek. She saw the sun already high in the sky. She heard snoring. The two children both had their heads in her lap. She smiled and gently touched their heads. "Sweet children."

The woman next to her smiled. "You slept good. The children like you."

Sofia nodded. "They are like . . ." She didn't finish. How terrible a mother she was to leave her children behind.

"I'm Ana. It's a hard trip for the little ones. You'll bring them later."

A tear tracked down Sofia's face, and she swiped it away. "Yes, later. I'm Sofia. Where are we?"

"We just passed Dallas. We are going to St. Louis. We all have family there. You?"

"Washington, D.C. Is it near St. Louis?"

The driver glanced in the rearview mirror. "Sorry, lady, I only go to St. Louis. No time—and I'm sure you don't have the money to pay for a drive to Washington, D.C."

"I . . . I have . . ."

Ana grasped her arm. Sofia said no more.

Ana waited until the driver was in conversation with the other men in the front seat. "Do not reveal any money you have—especially if you're in the bus terminal. You may be able to get a ticket to Washington; but if you show too much money, they may steal it—or you."

Sofia opened her eyes wide. "Steal me?"

"They take women—make them work like slaves or sell them for sex."

Sofia's shoulders slumped, and she closed her eyes. "I thought America was friendly and helpful. Like you."

"Most people are, but there are a lot of bad ones, too,, especially if you're a woman by yourself. And you are small. It makes you look more vulnerable. You'll stay with my cousins, and we'll help you find a ride to Washington. You have children who miss you."

"Gracias, Ana."

"De nada, Sofia. We have food." She pulled out a block of cheese and a loaf of bread. She broke off a piece of each for everyone. The children had awakened and devoured the bit of food. "We only have a couple of jars of water, so we have to share."

Isobel's legs burned from hurrying. Her stomach clenched as she saw the headmaster about to close the school doors. She ran faster, tugging Manny along with her.

He scowled, then smiled. "Niños, you must try to get here earlier."

Isobel nodded. "Si, sir. We will try." She placed her hand on Manny's shoulder, a sign to say nothing. It would only cause trouble with Tía .

Children moved along in the hallways. Isobel pulled Manny behind her. She saw a few children hold their noses as they passed.

Rage rose in her, but she clamped her lips tight to keep the mean words inside. And hitting would only cause trouble. She breathed deeply. At least they had clothes to wear, even if they were thin, old, baggy, and smelly. Next time she had to scrub the floor, she would rinse their clothes first if Tía or the cousins weren't watching her. Tía wouldn't allow her to put hers or Manny's clothes in with the immediate family's clothes when she made her do the laundry.

"Bella, are you angry because I can't run as fast as you?" Manny's big eyes searched his sister's.

"No, Manny, I could never be mad at you. Never. Remember, when they give you food, try to hide a little in your pocket or just eat a lot. If Tía gets mad, we might not get supper. Now, here's your classroom. I'll see you later."

Isobel turned her thoughts to her own learning. Today, she would study triangles. Every subject topped her favorite list, but math was the most fun. Perhaps she could teach when she grew up. She could ignore the growls of her empty stomach until lunch time. She would be careful, then, because if the cousins saw her eat extra or hide food, they would tell on her to the teacher or to their mama. But one teacher, Señora Ramos, always smiled at her and sometimes gave her extra food. When Isobel and Manny weren't there for a few days, Señora Ramos inquired about their absence. Isobel confided only a little—that they had to work. Señora Ramos would nod and give her extra food.

"Bella, I'm cold."

"Come with me. We'll keep each other warm. If Tía gets mad too much, we'll run away."

"Could we run to Mama? I miss her. Tell me about her again."

She ruffled Manny's hair. "Oh, Manny, you remember."

"I know, but I like to hear you tell me."

Isobel scooted over on the thin mattress. There were no sheets—just a threadbare blanket—but at least they each had one. She pulled her brother close and then wrapped both blankets around them as best she could. In health class, Señora Ramos had said when people ate more food, they would make more energy and stay warmer at night. She had looked right at Isobel then. Maybe she knew their situation, though Isobel had never revealed the sparse accommodations or the miniscule amount of food they ate. Manny coughed a lot. She held him closer. He needed more to eat.

"Well, I remember when you were two and I was four. Mama and Papa were still married. Papa had sales to make; so he would pile us all into the car, and we would drive so many places. Sometimes, we would stop at a café for food; but usually, we would go to the parks at lunchtime and have a picnic. Mama was so pretty and had long black hair that she would tie back. Papa always liked her to just let it stay loose. So when the car windows were down, her hair would fly everywhere and would tickle our faces."

Manny giggled. "I think I remember her hair tickling me. Tell me more."

"Mama made the best quesadillas and would bring them along on those picnics, and we ate them cold. We would give some of it to the squirrels."

"I wish we had enough food now to give to the squirrels. Is Mama happy that we're here?" His lips were puckered again.

"Mama wanted us to stay with her cousin Marisa, but Marisa got sick."

"I wish Tía Luisa would get sick."

"Shhh, Manny, we don't want them to hear us."

"But don't you?"

Isobel giggled. "It would be nice."

"Then Mama would have to come back for us."

"Are you warmer now, Manny? We should get to sleep. Maybe Mama will call tomorrow."

"Bella, your hair is getting longer. I'm going to let it tickle my face and pretend it's Mama."

Isobel chuckled. "I could do the same with your hair, but you need a haircut."

Darkness engulfed the surroundings by the time the station wagon limped into the city. A flat tire had derailed them for an hour, but it provided time to stretch their legs, a welcome relief. Sofia had not seen so many lights in a city in her life. Most of her life was in small towns in Bolivia. She'd made a few trips with her husband to the city, but the lights of St. Louis outdid all the lights she'd ever seen.

Ana insisted she enter her cousin's home with her. She was welcomed and given a mat on the floor to sleep. Grateful for a roof over her head and a place to stretch out with a blanket and a small pillow, she fell fast asleep. The crossing of the Rio Grande in the night and sleeping in the station wagon with damp clothes had not afforded her much rest.

Too soon, Ana nudged her awake. "Sofia, there is a bus to Washington, D.C., leaving in two hours. It stops in Chicago. You'll have to switch buses. It will arrive in Washington tomorrow morning at 7:00 a.m. You'll have to sleep on the bus, but that's better than trying to sleep in the bus terminal or arriving in the middle of the night. Do you have enough money? I might have some."

Sofia sat up and rubbed her eyes and stretched her neck. "Two hours. Okay. Thank you. Yes, I have enough. Wait, let me check. Do you know how much?"

Ana told her the amount, and she checked the secret wrap tied close to her midsection that housed her money.

"Yes, I have enough, and I can buy some food as well. I want also to give you some money for giving me a ride this far."

Ana pushed Sofia's hand down as she extended it with money. "No, you keep it. We are fine. You help another. Bring your babies to the States. But separate your funds. Keep your ticket money in one secure spot and your food money handy. Keep the rest hidden. The bad people out there will hurt you and take your money if they see it. Please be careful."

"Gracias, Ana. Perhaps I can use the bathroom to freshen up."

"Yes, it's right over there. I've already put some clean, dry clothes in there for you to wear. It's no problem, Sofia. Like I said, you help another. But be careful."

After Sofia returned from the bathroom, Ana and her cousin took her to the bus station and assisted her in finding the right route. They stayed with her until she stepped onto the bus. Sofia hugged her new friend before she climbed aboard.

Ana smiled. "Vaya con Dios, Sofia. Go with God. Perhaps we will meet again someday."

The tears blurred her eyes, and words caught in her throat. "Yes, yes" was all she could manage.

She hugged what few belongings she had to her stomach as she found a seat by the window. No one sat next to her, and she was glad of that. She needed to think. She would need to find a job. Ana had helped her send a telegram to her sister in Washington, D.C., notifying her of the arrival time. Camila had wanted to travel to the border to meet her but had no way. Perhaps Camila had found a place where she could work.

How long would it take to make enough to bring her children, her sweet ones, to the States? And how would she get them? What if she couldn't become a citizen quickly or make enough money? As she pondered the thoughts and fears that swirled in her mind, she fell fast asleep.

Awaking to the announcement that they had arrived in Chicago, Sofia quickly disembarked. Remembering Ana's cousin's instructions, she studied her ticket and found the number of the bus that would carry her the final leg of her journey. She had one hour and found a room in the station that had machines holding sandwiches and drinks. Again, Ana's cousin had shown her one before she left St. Louis and made sure she had coins to use.

She sat at a small table to eat. The table had not been wiped off, and stale coffee smells wafted all around. Ketchup and mustard stains graced the tabletop, and the wastebaskets overflowed with wrappers and napkins. On top of all that, human sweat assaulted her senses. Had she not had that chance to wash up at Ana's cousin's home, she would probably smell of fish herself. It was best to ignore all that. She had food, and she would be at her sister's early in the morning.

She boarded the bus; but this time, it was crowded. A man with a ratty coat and straggly hair sat next to her. She feared his smile was lecherous, so she held her measly belongings tightly on the window side and stared out the window. The man did not make conversation; but with him next to her, she didn't dare sleep and fought the urge to close her eyes.

The bus rode through business sections with buildings as tall as Sofia had ever seen. A wide expanse of water with great waves was off to the side. People in the seat behind her commented that it was Lake Michigan. She shivered, recalling the fright of being almost swept away in the Rio Grande.

Then they traveled higher on a bridge. As she stared down at the water far below next to congested roadways, Sofia felt her heart in her throat. The sweat that poured out of her forehead slid down her face. She had to close her eyes. It was too much. How would she survive this trip?

When she afforded a glance at the man next to her, he flashed a positively evil grin. Sofia narrowed her eyes and met his gaze until he turned away. Weakness could not be seen in her. That would lead to being taken advantage of, and that could not happen. True, she was small, but toughness dwelt in her every cell. She had determined long ago to make a better life for herself and her children.

CHAPTER THREE

The bus pulled into Union Station in Washington, D.C., right on time. Sofia stared out the window and allowed everyone to leave before her. She didn't know why. Exhaustion? Fear? Amazement at the size of the building? The numbers of bustling people? How would she find her way to the right spot to meet Camila? Nervousness and fear rose in her, but she must blot it out so that she did not fall victim to the people Ana had warned her about. She needed to look like she knew exactly where to go.

She paused upon seeing a restroom. As she turned to enter, a young girl exited. Sofia gazed at her—so pretty and sweet, with long dark curls and about the same age as Isobel. A stab of pain entered her heart. She missed her children so much.

Then a flash of dark clothing rushed past her. A man snatched the girl, slapping his hand over her mouth and wrapping his arm around her middle. Her panicked eyes bore into Sofia. He ran out the nearest door.

Sofia stood aghast as the side door of a van slid open and the man with the girl jumped in.

The van sped off as a woman came out of the bathroom.

"Olivia? Olivia?" She studied the area, her eyes growing wider by the moment.

Sofia saw the panic rising in the woman. She pointed. "A man grabbed a girl and ran to a van. They are gone." Sofia covered her mouth, and tears rolled down her cheeks.

The woman screamed and fell to the floor. Sofia ran to her and helped her stand. "You must find police. You must." She saw an officer and waved. As the man arrived, Sofia told him what she had seen as the woman sobbed.

"Olivia, my baby, my baby." The woman grabbed the policeman.

"We'll do all we can, ma'am." He turned to Sofia. "What can you tell me about the man?"

Sofia shook. Would she be found out? "It happened so quickly." She darted her eyes. *I need to focus.* "He was tall and young, with shoulder-length hair. Dark leather jacket. Black pants. The van was gray. I . . . I don't remember anything else."

"You've been a big help." He spoke into a handheld radio, repeating what Sofia had told him.

Sofia jerked her head around. "Wait, there was a big gash in the side of the van, near the back. And the rear light was broken." How had she even noticed that?

The officer spoke again into his radio. He turned to Sofia. "That's incredibly helpful. Thank you. Here's my card. If you remember anything else, please call me."

Nodding her head upon taking the card, she turned to leave.

Olivia's mama reached out and touched her arm, tears streaming down her face. "Thank you. I cannot live without my daughter. She just walked out of the bathroom ahead of me. I paused to wipe out the sink and followed her. If you . . . if you hadn't seen her taken, I would never have known." She fell into Sofia's arms. "If I had just made her wait . . ." Her voice was engulfed in sobs.

The officer pulled her out of Sofia's arms. "Ma'am, we need you to give us information about your daughter; so hopefully, we can find her." He hesitated. "You should know, these situations are not always . . . resolved."

The woman fell to the floor once more. Sofia helped the officer bring her to her feet. "I will hope and pray that you find your daughter, your Olivia."

The woman nodded, then convulsed once more with grief. The officer walked her away, talking softly.

Sofia wiped her hand across her eyes. Ana had said there were bad people. Should she have just stayed in Bolivia with her children? *Dear God, protect them. Please help this woman find her daughter.* Olivia's sweet face and her mother's horrified look would remain in her mind forever.

Sofia turned around. Which door should she leave by to find Camila? She'd almost forgotten she needed to visit the restroom. Concern weighed heavily on her as she entered the bathroom.

Upon washing her hands, she splashed her face and studied it in the mirror. Her hair was almost as straggly as that man's on the bus. She wet her hands and smoothed her dark hair. Her deep brown eyes held weariness. Smoothing her dress, she was glad Isobel had inherited her papa's slimness, even though Manny had received her shortness and stockiness. She glanced around and saw that no one was nearby. She practiced looking confident, an expression that had fled with Olivia's kidnapper.

When satisfied she could safely exit the bus station, she proceeded to do just that. She scanned the many faces and did not see her sister. Ten minutes later, she tried exiting a door on the opposite side of Union Station.

"Sofia, Sofia, mi amor, there you are! I've been waiting thirty minutes. Are you okay?" Camila ran to Sofia and embraced her. "You've had a long journey. Let's go. My car is right over there. You can tell me all about it once we're on our way."

Buildings loomed on every side of the hectic highway. Car horns blared, and stoplights interfered with travel every few blocks. None of the roads went in a straight line.

Sofia groaned. "So many cars and so many people. Is it always this busy here? How do you rest?"

Camila reached across and patted her hand. "You're tired. It's hectic here, but you'll get used to it. I see concern in your eyes. Did all go well? How are the children?"

Sofia wrung her hands and shook her head. "The children are okay, but . . . " She stretched her neck and swiped at a tear. "Camila, oh, Camila, it was so hard. Luisa wouldn't let me come to see them, so I've been without them since you and I left. I am a terrible mother."

"No! You have finally made it here safe and sound. You will send for them soon. You trust Luisa and Victor, si?"

"Si. But I know Luisa can be hard at times. She was hesitant about the cost of feeding them. I promised they are good children and would help her in every way. But still, I worry."

Camila stopped the car at a stoplight and turned to face Sofia. "Ah, you'll have a job soon. You'll send money to help and save enough to bring them here."

Sofia nodded. "Yes, I suppose."

Camila flashed her a smile as the light changed. "I already have a possible place for you to work. It is a hotel not far from my house. They need housekeepers. You'll clean rooms, maybe laundry."

"That will be good. I'm ready to work. I can clean and do laundry. I am strong."

"First, you must rest from your journey. Was it hard?"

Sofia chewed her bottom lip before responding. "I almost drowned, but a man saved me. And then a woman, Ana, took me to St. Louis and helped me get bus fare to here. I wouldn't have made it without them. But they told me there are plenty of bad people here in the States. A terrible man sat next to me on the bus . . . "

"Oh no, did he try anything?"

"No, but he looked like he wanted to. I had to stare him down, and then he turned away. It was scary."

"You always were tough. That's good, Sofia."

"But, oh, Camila, here at the bus station, a young girl—probably ten years old at the most—walked out of the bathroom before her mom came out, and a young man grabbed her and carried her off. He threw her into a van and drove away. The poor mother just collapsed. The police came, but . . . I'm still shaking. I'm so scared for that little girl, and I was afraid the policeman would ask for my identification papers."

Camila shook her head. "It's in the news every week of children being kidnapped. And they just disappear. No one—on the news, anyway—says anything, but I've heard rumors that they are sold for sex. It's so horrible."

Sofia gasped. "Should I bring my children here? Will they be safe?"

"Hold them close when they come. We all must watch out for the little ones. It's happening in Bolivia, too, dear one. Cousin Selena keeps me informed. It is good to get them here under your watchful eye. And we will get you a green card as soon as we can, so you can work. That will be your identification. And, dear one, you'll find most people here are kind and helpful."

CHAPTER FOUR

April 1981

"Hector, my man! How are you today?"

"I'm good. And you, Freddy?"

The young man behind the hotel check-in desk ran his hand through his black hair. "Better than good. Did you see those blue skies out there? I get off in two hours and got a new girl going for a ride in my Mustang."

Hector laughed. "Well, you have fun. I'm here till seven today."

"Hector, Hector, I have good news for you. We just hired a brand new señorita today. And she's a looker. I think she's just your type."

Hector shook his head. "Freddy, get back to work."

Freddy leaned on the counter and lowered his voice. "I'm telling you, I should get a finder's fee. I think she's the perfect woman for you."

Hector waved his hand as if he were swatting a bug. "Stop. I don't go after women like you. Make sure you treat this gal tonight with respect."

Freddy guffawed. "Aww, you know I'm a nice guy. But, Hector, Hector . . . " He waggled his finger for Hector to come close.

Hector sighed and stepped closer to the counter.

Freddy whispered, "She's from Bolivia, Hector, just like you. She's a Bolivian babe, I'm telling you. Cute, no, close to gorgeous. Tiny. Long black hair and the biggest brown eyes. Just what you need."

"I'm sure we'll meet sometime. Now, we both have work to do. Tell me the rooms that are having shower problems."

After Freddy gave him the room numbers, Hector walked down the hall, shaking his head all the way. At the end of the hall, he pulled out his keys to open the door to the maintenance closet and grabbed a tool bag.

As he climbed the steps to the third floor, he mumbled, "A Bolivian babe. That Freddy."

He pulled out his key to enter room 304 when a pretty woman stepped out.

Hector backed up. "Forgive me, I'm maintenance to fix the shower faucet. Is this a good time? I can come back later."

The woman looked down, allowing her jet black hair to fall in her face. She pushed it back. "It is okay. I'm so sorry. I just started today, and I forgot to put the clean towels in this room. The people aren't here right now."

Hector said nothing. He just stared. The description of beautiful fit her, and he could detect the Bolivian accent.

The woman's eyes opened wide. Those eyes were amazing. Then she hung her head and mumbled, "So sorry. So sorry," and hurried down the hallway, while attempting to tie her hair back with an elastic band.

"Wait. Wait. Forgive me, miss."

She stopped and turned around and scrunched her face, revealing her confusion. "It is okay."

Hector set his tool bag down and approached her. "You just started today?"

She nodded. "Si, yes."

"Welcome. I'm Hector, the maintenance man. I'm here most days if you have any questions."

She smiled. "Thank you. My name is Sofia. I'm happy to be working."

Hector nodded and couldn't think of anything else to say, so he just kept nodding and walked backward to Room 304. He thought he heard her stifle a giggle. But Freddy was right. She was a babe.

He grabbed his bag and went into the room. He began shaking his head. "I am such a dunce. She saw me acting smitten." Then he smiled. "I wonder if she's available. She's from Bolivia. What are the odds?"

He was still smiling when his shift ended at seven. He sighed in relief that the second shift check-in guy was behind the counter, not Freddy, when he left. Perhaps tomorrow, he'd see Sofia again. Sofia—what a pretty name.

"Isobel, why did you not peel more potatoes?" Tía Luisa gave the girl a withering look.

"There were only those, Tía." Isobel felt her neck tighten and braced herself.

"What?" She grabbed Isobel's shoulders. "Why didn't you get more when I sent you to the store?"

"I got what you . . . " Isobel saw the anger in Tía's eyes. "I'm sorry, Tía Luisa."

"Now, get to the market before it closes and get me enough. Cousin Selena and her family are coming for dinner."

"Oh, that's nice."

Tía slapped her. "I don't need your approval. I need your obedience. Now get."

Isobel ran out, almost tripping, blinded by the tears from the sting and the rebuke. She wiped her face as she slowed down but maintained a rapid pace. Rounding the bend before the store, she almost plowed into Cousin Selena.

"Bella, Bella, how are you? We are a little early, so everyone is just walking around in the little shops." She placed a hand on Bella's shoulder and lifted her chin with her finger. "Baby, what is wrong? Why the tears? What is the red on your face?"

Bella dissolved into tears against Selena.

Selena pulled her over to a bench. "Tell me."

The girl told of the incident that had just happened.

"Oh, child, Luisa can be short-tempered. I'm sure she was just trying to have everything ready on time."

Bella raised her eyes to meet Selena's eyes. "Cousin, she is mean. We don't have enough food. We are cold at night. We have to do all the chores. And we have to use the outside toilet."

Selena gasped. "Now, Bella, you must not tell stories when you are upset. But I will look around tonight, maybe ask a few questions. But now, wipe your face and get those potatoes."

Hector generally avoided the breakroom when the cleaning ladies were there. He valued peace and quiet, and the laughter and silliness that filled the room sent him outdoors or to another spot in the hotel. He would chuckle at their antics, but it wasn't his favorite place. Why, then, did he discover himself checking his watch and wandering in toward the end of their break? Sofia seemed to draw him like a moth was pulled toward the light.

The girls always said hi and smiled at Hector but really paid him no mind. He stood in front of the cooler trying to decide what he wanted, but what he desired was a conversation with Sofia. She hung back as if it took her a long time to clean up her lunch items. She would look down, then tilt her face toward Hector and smile. He nodded, grabbed a soda, and left.

The third day, she smiled again. "Hi, I forgot your name."

Hector faced her and grinned. "Hector. You're Sofia? We met your first day."

She wagged her head. "Yes, yes, so many names and things to remember."

"I'm happy to assist if you need anything. Do let me know if you notice anything amiss. I'm in charge of maintenance, so I can help fix it."

She gathered her things and exited the breakroom, casting a quick glance back at Hector. Did her eyes sparkle? How is that possible? Hector looked around as if to orient himself to the location. He let out a deep breath and closed his eyes. *Goodness, she rattles me.*

Two days slipped by before Manny and Isobel arrived in the schoolyard. Tía Luisa had kept them busy with constant chores and not allowed them to attend. Students huddled in the playground whispering.

As the two walked toward the group, Maria broke off from the gathering. "It's not Bella or Manny, everyone."

Isobel scrunched her face. "What's not us?"

"We heard that one of our classmates was stolen."

"Stolen?"

Maria lowered her voice and widened her eyes. "Taken for terrible things."

Señora Ramos walked into the playground. "Isobel, so good to see you and Manny. Please come here. Maria, I think it's time to join the others and get to class."

"Si, Señora."

Isobel stared after Maria. "She said someone was stolen. Did they think it was me?"

Señora Ramos wrapped her arm around the girl's shoulders. "We worried that it might be you or your brother." She looked behind her. "Manny, come with us. Isobel, the streets are becoming more dangerous. You must be even more careful coming to school and going home. Does your family realize that the roads are very unsafe for children?"

"Tía often walks with our cousins to school, but we have to do the dishes and sweep the house before we leave. We don't get to go with them."

Señora Ramos stopped and turned to Isobel. "That's why you're often late?"

Isobel nodded and let her hands hang at her side. "And if the job isn't good enough, we are kept home from school."

Señora Ramos bent down so that she was eye to eye. "Young lady, I want you to try to get up a little earlier, so you have everything done well. And then you can walk with your tía and cousins to school on time. Can you do that? It will be so much safer."

Isobel swiped at a tear sliding down her cheek and turned her head. "I'll . . . I'll try . . . but . . ."

Manny stepped closer. "Tía doesn't want us to walk with them. She doesn't like us." He kicked the dirt. "I don't like her either. Maybe Bella and I will run away."

"Oh, Manny." Señora Ramos pulled him into an embrace. "Promise me, Manny. You won't let Isobel run away, and you won't run either."

Manny pulled back and dragged his arm across his nose, gathering mucus all over his wrist. Señora Ramos stood and pulled a cloth from her pocket. "Here, wipe your nose and arm. Then go inside to the washroom and clean up. Isobel and I will be right in."

Isobel watched as Manny trudged into the school building. "Señora Ramos, who got stolen?"

Her teacher sighed deeply. "Did you know Alejandra?"

Isobel gasped and covered her mouth with her hands. Her stomach lurched, and tears threatened to cascade down her cheeks. She often played with Alejandra on the playground, and they both competed in the math contests. Tears welled in her eyes. "Is she found? Can they get her back?"

Señora wrapped her arm around the girl's shoulders once more. "I talked with her parents this morning, and they have talked to the police. Stolen kids are rarely found. If you know how to pray, you should pray for her."

"My mama taught me to pray before she left." Isobel's voice hitched. "I pray for my mama, and I will pray for Alejandra. Why did Maria think it was me?"

"We only found out about Alejandra yesterday, and you and Manny had not been in school for two days. Some thought it was you or Manny. Isobel, you must promise you won't run away. Getting stolen is a hundred times worse than what is happening with your tía. Do you understand me? I will help you as much as I can; but you must try to do what she expects, so you can come to school each day. Okay, Isobel?"

Everything turned blurry, and Isobel swiped at her face. "I should go to the washroom, too, Señora. Thank you for talking to me."

"Just be careful, Isobel."

CHAPTER FIVE

May 1981

The phone rang. Manny stood up. "Bella, maybe it's Mama."

Cousin Gina appeared at the door. "Come to the phone. It's your mama."

Manny ran with Isobel right behind. He grabbed the phone. "Mama, Mama, I miss you."

Mama's voice crackled back. "I miss you, too, Manny. Can you hear me okay?"

Tía Luisa took the phone from Manny. "Sofia, the connection isn't too good, but your niños are just fine. Here's Isobel." She handed the phone to Isobel while raising her eyebrows and staring at the girl. Her whisper could only be heard by the children. "You're doing just fine, si?"

"Hi, Mama, how are you?"

"I'm fine, baby. Is everything okay? I talked to Selena yesterday."

Once more, Tía grabbed the phone. "Yes, Selena came to visit. She does that every once in a while."

Tía continued chatting with Mama, relating that the children were attending school and doing well. Manny's big eyes kept searching Isobel's, but she just looked away.

"Say goodbye to your mama now. I'm sure she can't afford to spend a long time on the telephone."

Isobel took the phone and turned away from Tía. "Goodbye, Mama. We miss you."

She handed the phone to Manny. He closed his eyes and sighed. "Mama, when can you come and get us? I don't like—"

Tía grabbed the phone. "Manny doesn't always like all the good vegetables we cook for him. He's adjusting well, though. And thank you for the money. It helps provide good food for the children. Thank you for calling, Sofia." Tía ended the call and narrowed her eyes at Isobel and Manny. "For that comment, Manny, you two will miss supper tonight. You are being well taken care of, and that is what your mama is paying for. You will let her know how much you appreciate it the next time she calls. Now, go do the laundry."

Isobel and Manny carried water to the huge pot in the side yard, sparsely populated with weedy grass. "I hate her, Isobel. Why is she so mean?"

She stopped, and the water in the bucket sloshed. "Shh, Manny. You can't say that. If she hears that, she'll just send us away."

"We could live in the dump where we play sometimes. There are things there that we could use to make a little house. It'd be as good as we have here. And I've seen kids beg for food, and they get some. We wouldn't even have to be late for school." Manny lifted his chin. "We could do that."

Isobel dumped the water in the barrel and set the bucket in the dirt. She shook her head at Manny. "We might be able to do that, but I've heard that kids get stolen while they're in the dump. I know we play there, but it's not safe if you're by yourself."

Manny stopped. He narrowed his eyes. He set his buckets down and fisted his hands while staring at the ground. He exhaled deeply through his nose. "So, when that man grabbed José last week, he was stolen? I thought it was his papa or tío. I haven't seen him since and just thought he got in trouble." He swiped a tear on his cheek. He looked up at his sister. "He's gone? Stolen? He was my friend. But we wouldn't let that happen to us because we'd be together, right? We'd be safe."

Tía's voice rang out. "Are you going to do the laundry or just stand there talking? I can add a whipping if that's needed."

Isobel's eyes warned Manny. "We have work. Let's get it done. I want to go to school tomorrow."

Good permeated the day. Isobel didn't understand it, but lightheartedness occupied her being. She trembled as she thought about it, somewhat fearful it would flee. No, she would enjoy it as long as she could. She sensed Manny felt the same. He'd started skipping a few feet in front of her.

Tía Luisa had allowed them to accept an invitation from Señora Ramos to attend church. Joy emanated from this church. Everyone seemed happy. The worship songs made her tingle. Such happiness shone in the faces as they sang. She understood very little of what the pastor said, but his love for everyone and for God was almost tangible. She felt it. And a knowledge secured her heart. God loved her and would take care of her and Manny. She prayed this confidence would never leave. *Don't worry about that now. Just enjoy it.*

A picnic ensued after the service. Señora Ramos told the children they were welcome and that she had brought extra food for them. They stayed just long enough to have a few bites to eat, but Isobel knew Tía Luisa would expect them home shortly after the service. So she caught up to her brother; and they skipped home hand in hand, humming the worship tunes they'd heard at church.

As they arrived around the corner from home, Isobel stopped. "Manny, we must walk now and be very obedient to Tía when we arrive. We can't be giddy."

"Why does she not want us to be happy?"

"I don't know. But let's just do our best. Okay?"

Manny nodded.

Upon entering the gate, it seemed too quiet. Isobel opened the door and found no one home. A note lay on the table. "We've gone for a family picnic. Wash the kitchen floor while we're gone and fold the clothes." Isobel placed the note back on the table. "Hmm. I guess we'd better get busy."

Manny nodded and grabbed the bucket to fill with water. "We could have stayed for the church picnic, and they'd never know."

"True. Unless the floor wasn't washed before they arrived."

Isobel knelt and scrubbed the floor with a rag that she dipped in the soapy water in the bucket. Manny followed with a clean-water rag to remove any soapy residue. Then they both dried the floor with a different set of rags. After dumping the water, they hung the rags on the clothesline in the side yard.

Laughing tumbled into the house as the family trailed in. No one said a word to Isobel or Manny for several minutes.

Their cousin Gina peeked into their room. "What fun we had. Mama said she would have brought you along, but you wanted to go to church. Oh well."

Isobel detected the smirk in her voice.

Gina didn't remain for a response but giggled as she left their room.

Isobel's heart determined to sink. Manny's eyes brimmed with tears. She drew him into an embrace. "No, we will not be sad or cry. We learned today that God loves us. It will be okay . . . even if it isn't." She sighed. "You know, even if we stayed home from church, she would have found a reason to not let us go."

Manny stood and kicked the wall. "You're right. I'm glad we went to church." Then he faced his sister. "But if we get to go again, let's stay for the picnic . . . even if we get in trouble."

Isobel smiled. "I bet she just let us go so they could go somewhere without us." She looked sideways and grinned at Manny. "Maybe that means we can go again."

As the day went by and the family didn't speak to them and only shared a small amount of their dinner with them, Isobel's heart descended toward sadness. There was so much to be sad about: their treatment from Tía Luisa and the cousins, the lack of food and warmth when cold, and most of all, missing Mama.

But then she heard a voice. Where was it? She listened every which way before it dawned on her that the voice came from within. It was soft but strong. *Don't be sad, Isobel. I'll take care of you.*

It was so strange, yet so comforting—and believable. She'd ask Señora Ramos about it before she told Manny.

CHAPTER SIX

June 1981

Hector noticed it more and more at his hotel—middle-aged men and young girls. His insides rumbled with unrest. The obvious scenario sent his mind reeling. But what could he do?

One day, he walked past the check-in desk on his way to the breakroom. A balding man sporting a pouchy stomach stood with a teenage girl at the counter. Freddy glanced at the girl and back to the man. Hector thought the man stiffened at Freddy's gaze.

He gave Freddy a gritty stare. "My teenager has never been to the D.C. area before. We have so many places to see."

Freddy smiled. "Well, you've come to the right place. We have shuttles to the downtown area for just a small fee. There is so much to see. Be sure to let me know if there is anything I can do to help. We have several brochures about all the sites to visit." He laid several on the counter. "There are more over there." He pointed to the nearby rack stacked full of pamphlets touting the variety of locations to enjoy.

The girl dropped her eyes as the man grabbed the brochures and gripped her arm. He led her to the elevator. The uneasiness that emanated from the girl kept Hector from moving. Her unkempt long blond hair somehow betrayed the man's comments of fatherhood.

Hector wanted to grab her and run, call the police, punch the man—do something, but what?

Freddy watched them, then looked at Hector and shook his head.

Hector looked around and, seeing no one in the lobby, walked over to the counter. "Freddy, I think we both know what's happening here."

Freddy nodded and whispered, "That's the fourth one in two weeks. I don't know what to do. I called the police once; but because I didn't have any solid evidence, they couldn't do anything."

Hector motioned for Freddy to follow him into the breakroom. Nobody was there. They sat so Freddy could see if anyone came to check in. Hector got a soda out of the cooler. "We must do something. Do you think we can help these girls?"

Freddy sighed and rubbed his face. "I've heard that attempts to help are really dangerous. The people who are behind this are ruthless. You don't want to mess with them."

Hector popped the can open and took a sip. "I know, but these girls need assistance."

Sofia walked in and gave a sweet smile to Hector. "I heard you. You have to be careful talking like that."

Hector and Freddy just stared at Sofia.

Sofia came close, lowering her voice. Her nearness sent shivers down Hector's back. "The cleaning girls have already been talking. We've put together a plan we'd like to try. We were trying to figure out how to get you two to help." She grinned. "But it seems you might want to join us."

Hector stood and walked to the door to see if anyone was around to overhear them, but he went mainly to break the spell of the growing attraction to Sofia. No one occupied the lobby. He returned to the table. He tried to avoid looking in her eyes. They were beautiful eyes, bright but slightly shadowed. "What's your plan?"

Sofia sat at the table and addressed Freddy. "Always put them on an upper floor. As soon as they get to the room, call the man back to the lobby. Their credit card didn't go through, or the maintenance man"—she smiled at Hector—"said the AC or something isn't working right, and they have to change rooms. As soon as he gets on the elevator, one of the cleaning ladies goes in with the laundry cart and hides the girl, covered with towels and sheets, and goes to a different room. Always keep a room open that we can use."

Hector let out a big breath. "He'll bring the girl with him."

Sofia hung her head. "Maybe wait a few minutes and he'll leave her, secure her in the room so she can't escape."

Freddy shook his head. "Even if that works, he'll call the police because his so-called daughter has disappeared."

Sofia clapped her hands. "No, he doesn't want to deal with the police."

Hector chewed his lower lip. "That might work. But where do we take the girls?"

"Two of the cleaning ladies rent rooms in a big house. The owners belong to a church a few blocks from here that is helping other girls and little boys."

Freddy's eyes opened wide. "Boys?"

"Yes." Sofia's eyes welled up. "Little boys. It's awful, but they've been able to rescue some children and then provide families—or, at least, support for them. I have two little ones back in Bolivia with family, but that is my biggest fear for them. I hope to be able to get them soon."

"That must be hard." Hector reached out to pat her hand but pulled it back. *She has children. A husband? Is she running from something?*

The elevator door dinged open. Freddy returned to the counter. Hector and Sofia peeked out the door. It was the man who'd just brought in the girl.

"How may I help you, sir?" His voice held no suspicion that Hector could notice.

"Oh, my wife called. We have a minor emergency at home and need to go now. So, we must check out. Thank you so much. Right, sweetie?" He tightened his grip on the girl's arm.

Freddy studied her. "I'm sorry you'll miss out on your plans." His voice was soft.

The girl glanced up and met Freddy's eyes. Hector could see the pain on her face and assumed Freddy did as well.

The man slapped the key on the counter. "Let's go. And don't worry, I won't be requesting a refund." He marched to the door and exited the building.

Sofia slumped in her chair as Freddy re-entered the breakroom. "We lost her."

"I know." Freddy hit the wall with his fist.

Hector sat down. "That poor girl. He just used her and now will probably pass her on to someone else."

Sofia shook her head. "Or keep her for more of the same. Did you see her face? She's hopeless. And we did nothing." A tear tracked down her cheek.

"We need to have a good plan. How will we signal each other?"

Sofia took a deep breath. "Okay, I think all the cleaning girls are on board. We all have seen this or have people that could be kidnapped like this. Freddy, can you and Hector signal each other easily?"

"I have a pager, so Freddy can let me know." Hector paused and stared at a corner of the room. "But he has to let me know as soon as he suspects because I might be in a repair that I can't leave." He shook his head. "Okay, how about this? If a man and girl come in, he'll page me—maybe a special code. And if I'm tied up, I'll have a code response . . . one for 'I need time' and one for 'I'm available.' If I need time, he'll take longer for the check in. Can you do that, Freddy? Stall the check-in?"

Freddy grinned. "I can pretend I have a complicated phone call I'm taking care of at the moment. It often happens, and people just have to wait."

"Can the cleaning ladies have pagers?"

"I think that's a good idea. And we have extra ones. I'll ask the boss."

"What if he's not against what these people are doing?"

"Well, we'll just approach it in the interest of efficiency. At least one cleaning lady per shift should have a pager."

Sofia nodded. "That would work because we already have ways to communicate if we need help from each other. And we usually work in pairs, so one can alert the others while one gets the girl. We'll always have a room ready to take the girl." She sighed. "What if the boss or other guests see or figure out what's going on?"

Freddy let out a big breath. His eyes darted around the room. "I may have to let the boss know."

"He could shut us down before we start." Hector tossed his can in the recycling bin.

"True. Let's just see how it works. We could get fired."

Sofia lifted her chin. "There are other hotels where we could work if that happens." She glanced at each of them. "But we have to do this, don't you agree?"

Both Freddy and Hector nodded.

Freddy stood and then sat back down. "Wait, what about the later shifts? We don't have cleaning ladies on in the evening. I'm sometimes here till eleven for check-in but not cleaning."

Sofia rubbed her neck. "I'm willing to work later, but most cleaning is morning to mid-afternoon. Talk to your boss and see if some of us could be on a later shift, maybe cleaning the lobby or something."

Freddy rested his chin in his hand. "Okay, I'll find out. If we're going to do this, we need to be here for some of the later check-ins."

Hector stood. "I'm here late sometimes. That's okay for me. But I have to get back to work now. Let's talk more later."

Isobel carried the ribbon close to her heart. She'd won a math contest at school; and everyone had cheered, even the kids who'd made fun of her clothes. The acceptance and accolades of the other students rang in her mind as she rehearsed all the way home the moment of winning and the cheers. Life actually seemed good.

"Tell me again what happened, Bella. Can I hold your ribbon?"

Isobel handed the ribbon to him and with grand gestures retold the story. "It was so close. I thought I'd lost because I got one problem wrong. But Andres got it wrong, too, so we had one more try. I got it right; and Andres missed it, so I won. Everyone stood and clapped. Andres shook my hand. He wasn't even mad that I won."

"We should celebrate, Bella. Let's stop and play at the dump. Maybe we'll find a doll for you to play with."

Isobel smiled and took Manny's hand. "Yes, let's do that. But maybe we'll find a truck for you." They both started skipping.

Thirty minutes later, they arrived home, laughing. No trucks, no dolls, but they'd joined other kids playing baseball with a stick for a bat and a bag of wire for a ball.

The laughter thudded to a halt when they met Tía at the gate. Isobel regained her smile and reached out her ribbon. "Look, Tía, I won a math contest."

"Why are you late? Where have you been?"

"Well, we—"

"Enough." Tía slapped Isobel's arm, and the ribbon drifted to the ground. "Get to the store. Once more, you have not followed directions in getting more potatoes."

"You never told me to—"

Tía's hand met Isobel's face. The sting would create a red welt on her cheek but would probably be gone by the time she returned to school—if Tía would let them return.

Tía shoved money into her hand, and Isobel and Manny turned to go to the store. "No, Manny. You need to stay here and sweep." She grabbed his arm and turned back to the house.

Isobel looked back. Manny's lips were puckered and his hands in fists. Once Tía and Manny were inside, she ran and picked up her now-soiled ribbon. She stuffed it in her pocket and hurried to the store, swiping away the tears that blurred her eyes.

"Why, Isobel, is that you? Are you crying? What's wrong?"

Isobel jerked to a stop. There was Cousin Selena again. She flew into her arms and sobbed. "It's awful, Cousin. Tía Luisa is so mean. I want to just run away."

Selena lifted her chin. "Isobel, this is the second time I've seen you like this. Is it really that bad? Are you just having a hard time in school and missing your mama?"

Isobel's chest heaved, and she let out a gasping breath, trying to control her weeping. "No, Cousin, I love school. I just won a math contest. I do miss Mama, but . . . "

"Tell me, child. I will call your mama."

Isobel shook her head. "No. When she calls, Tía Luisa and the cousins gather around; and we cannot tell her the truth. We must tell her all is well."

Selena stepped back and placed her hands on Isobel's shoulders. "I will inform your mama, and Luisa will not know that we know. Now, go to the store quickly. I will be there for dinner, but Luisa will not know that we have talked. You understand?"

Isobel nodded and ran to the store. Perhaps that voice she'd heard had to do with this. Cousin Selena would tell Mama. Maybe things would change.

Sofia's pager pinged. Her heart skipped a beat as she glanced at its face. The code seemed to blare at her. She was already on the same floor. She notified her cleaning partner.

"You get her, Sofia. Bring her to this room. I will pray."

Her feet froze to the floor, and her arms went limp. "I . . . I . . . "

Joanie peered out of the bathroom. "Go now!"

Sofia took a deep breath and eased the cart out of the room. A man strode into the elevator, impatience screaming from his face. She hurried to the elevator doors when she heard them close. Yes, he was going down. She pulled out her key and entered the room. At first, she saw no one; then she noticed a slight movement and a moan from the bed.

"Sweetheart, I'm going to help you."

A girl sat up, gripping the blanket to herself. He'd left her naked. Sofia swallowed the anger and reached out. "Quickly, climb in this basket. Where are your clothes?" The girl pointed, and Sofia grabbed them and put them in the cart. "Please climb in. I won't look, and I will cover you. But we must move fast."

The girl obeyed. Sofia threw towels and sheets on top. "Don't make a sound."

Sofia took deep breaths as she exited the room. She passed the elevator and saw it was almost back to their floor. She started to run. But when the doors opened, she walked slowly toward the room where her cleaning partner had the door ajar.

Sofia collapsed in the chair and covered her face. Her partner began to uncover the girl but stopped as they heard footsteps in the hallway. Sofia bounced up and began straightening the bed, while Joanie returned to the bathroom.

A man flung open the door.

Sofia turned, startled. "Can we help you, sir?"

He looked around the room. "Did you see a young girl in the hallway?"

"No, the vending machines are at the other end of the hall."

His face reddened, and his neck stiffened. "I looked there. Are you sure? Were you cleaning in room 804?"

"We only clean rooms that are unoccupied, sir."

He turned, then glanced back. "And you heard no one else in the hallway?"

Joanie stepped out of the bathroom. "I may have heard the door to the stairs open and close, but I was in here cleaning."

The man stomped to the nearby entrance to the stairs.

Sofia released a big breath. "Just wait, little one," she whispered.

Five eternal minutes later, the room phone rang. Sofia picked it up. Freddy informed her the man had stalked the lounge area, peeked into the single unlocked woman's bathroom, looked outside each exit, then slammed the room key on the desk and left the building. He watched him drive out of the parking lot. "But don't leave the room until your friends arrive. When they do, take her in the cart to the loading dock. Is she okay?"

"We'll stay with her, Freddy. Thank you."

They closed the door and locked it. Sofia gently lifted the towels and sheet off the girl. She sat up and shook. Sofia wrapped a clean towel around her. "Do not fear, little one. We will get you to a safe place. Here, let me help you climb out. You can go in the bathroom and get your clothes back on."

Joanie waited until the girl was in the bathroom and then shook her head. "She must only be ten or eleven, poor thing. I wanted to hit that man . . . or worse. You played your part so well, Sofia."

"I was so scared, but I had to be brave. If this were my daughter . . ."

The door to the bathroom opened, and the girl stood in its entrance dressed in a pretty blue dress but no shoes.

"Oh no, we forgot your shoes. Do we dare go back to the room and get them?"

"I'll call Freddy." Joanie went to the phone.

Sofia took the girl's hand. "You don't need to be afraid anymore. We can help you."

Joanie hung up the phone. "Freddy called our friends at the church, and they're on their way. I'll go retrieve the shoes." She smiled at the girl. "Can you tell us your name?"

"Ava. What will become of me now?"

"We have friends at a church that will pick you up and take you there. They have rooms where you can eat and sleep, and people who will help you find your family, and doctors who can help if you need it."

"Will the man—the men—return?" Her whole body shook as she asked the question.

"No, you will never have to see them again."

The child dissolved into tears. Sofia encircled her with her arms and prayed that someone kind was there for her own little girl and boy. She'd heard from Selena that Luisa might not be that person. *I need to get my niños here. Please, God.* Joanie exited the room to find Ava's shoes.

The people from the church came to take Ava within minutes of the call. Sofia and Joanie remained with her until they arrived. Joanie knew the ones who could provide for the girl.

The child clung to Sofia, hesitant to go with more unknowns. Sofia knelt in front of her. "It's okay, sweetie. They will help you find your family or a family who will love you." She glanced at Joanie's friends, who nodded. "This is what they do. Maybe they can help you locate other girls. I will pray for you every day. Your awful life is over. It will get better." She gently pulled from her embrace. "Now go, Ava. May it be well with you."

Ava tentatively walked away with the couple, glancing back at Sofia and giving a little wave as she got into their van.

Sofia stood and stared as they drove away. Numbness had enveloped her, and she couldn't move.

Joanie tapped her shoulder, and she startled. "You stay here as long as you need. I'll go back up and get cleaning. The others are covering our rooms, so we don't get in any trouble."

Sofia nodded. After Joanie left, she whispered, "Dear God, take care of little Ava. No child should suffer this way." Pain gripped her stomach, and she almost doubled over. "My children shouldn't suffer having to be without their mama." Tears dripped off her chin. "Help Ava find the right family and please help my children to be okay until I can bring them safely here."

An hour later, the cleaning was finished; and several of the cleaners headed to the breakroom. As they entered, Freddy and Hector stood and clapped.

Freddy lifted his soda can. "You did it. Cheers! What a team!" He shook his head. "May any more of these situations that come our way be as successful."

Hector spread his arms. "It's magnificent. That girl can have a life again."

Before he knew it, Sofia ran into his open arms and wrapped her arms around him. "I was so scared, but I had to help her." Tears coursed down her cheeks.

Hector widened his eyes and placed his arms tentatively around Sofia. "It's okay. You were fantastic." He patted her back and tried not to gulp. He was holding Sofia in his arms, and everyone was watching.

Freddy grinned and winked. He mouthed the words, "Told you. Bolivian babe just for you."

Joanie looked from Freddy to Hector and giggled.

Sofia pulled away and swiped at her eyes. She glanced at Hector. "Umm, thank you." Her wide eyes turned to Joanie. "I think I'll eat my lunch. I forgot."

The four of them sat at the table, eating and drinking, rehearsing every detail of the day.

Joanie and Sofia checked out and left the hotel together, stopping at a café not far away to eat dinner. Joanie lowered her chin and looked up at Sofia with a sly grin. "Are you sweet on Hector? He certainly seems attracted to you."

"Oh, I don't know. It's hard to think about that now. I have too many things to be concerned about—not dating. He is cute, though, with that unruly curly hair. And his eyes are so kind . . . and such a pretty shade of brown."

Joanie grinned. "Not to mention, he's only two or three inches taller than you. I mean, he's short, but very muscular. Did you feel his muscles when he hugged you? Well, when you ran into his arms?"

Sofia hung her head. "I can't believe I did that." She smiled. "But, yes, he's very muscular."

Isobel saw Señora Ramos sitting on a bench, watching the children play. "May I sit with you, Señora?"

"You certainly may. How are you doing?" Her teacher, her friend, demonstrated such kindness to her in just her voice. Why was Tía Luisa's voice always so harsh?

Isobel hung her head. "May I ask a question?"

Señora Ramos placed a finger under the girl's chin and lifted it. "Sweetheart, this is school. This is the place for questions."

"But it's not about school."

Her teacher smiled. "That's okay. What's your question?"

"Well, the last time we were at church, Tía still got mad. I'd been so happy, and then I was so sad. I heard a voice. It was inside me, but it wasn't me." Isobel twisted the hem of her skirt in her fingers and peered at her teacher.

"What did the voice say?" Señora Ramos laid her hand on Isobel's busy fingers.

Isobel felt her heartbeat race. "It said . . . well, it told me not to be sad and that it—they, he, I don't know who—would take care of me."

Señora Ramos gave her a quick hug. "Oh, young lady, that's wonderful. I'm sure the voice belonged to God. He often speaks on the inside of us. Never forget what you heard. Trust God to help you when things don't go well."

The bell sounded, indicating the end of playtime.

Señora Ramos stood. "Isobel, always know I'm praying for you but really know that God will help you."

Isobel nodded. "Thank you." She skipped into school. Surely, things would get better.

The day after the rescue of Ava, Freddy, Hector, Joanie, and Sofia found themselves especially busy. Sensing a need to make up for lost time and worrying whether they should tell the boss all their details, they each buried themselves in work. Hector didn't see Sofia until he noticed her leaving for the day. She smiled and gave a little wave. He wanted to run after her and ask her out, but he was in the middle of vacuuming the lounge area. Stopping would be frowned upon. He saw Freddy watching him and chuckling.

Freddy shook his head and turned away. Everything about this woman called to him. Feeling her in his arms was so nerve-wracking, yet it rang true. Right. Meant to be. Could she be the one? He didn't know much about her, but did that matter? Maybe a little. She did have children. If she was married, that would change everything. He should find out. He hoped she was single, so he could ask her out.

The following day, Hector discovered Sofia had the day off. His heart sank.

Freddy noticed. He noticed everything. "Are you disappointed the B.B. is absent today? That would make a good nickname, a little love expression. B.B. for Bolivian Babe. You should make your move, man, as soon as she's back to work. There might be a lot of guys chasing her already. But really, Hector, she certainly seems to be drawn to you."

Hector stretched his neck, then shrugged his shoulders. "You really think so? I mean . . . well, I could . . . oh, I don't know." He could feel heat overtaking his face.

Freddy guffawed. "Oh, you *are* taken with her. I knew it. She'll be back tomorrow, but you're off. Want me to schedule you to be here, anyway?"

"I suppose."

"Done. Be here at ten." He laughed. "The boss already asked me if you might be able to work tomorrow. He wants a couple new AC units attached."

CHAPTER SEVEN

JULY, 1981

Olivia hung her head. Straggly strands of hair fell across her face. She wiped her eyes, though there were no more tears. Crying did no good and only exhausted her. Besides, Monica would slap her. The fight in her had diminished as well. Ricky just laughed when she fought his abuse of her. He called her feisty and handed her off to other men.

There remained no hope. The last time she'd been to church with Mama, the pastor had said that even in the darkest night, there was a dawn coming. But her dawns only meant pain and fear. Monica would jerk her out of bed with the other girls and hurry them into the shower, while Ricky watched and gloated. Breakfast consisted of a piece of bread and, if they were lucky, some cereal without milk. Then they were distributed. That's what Monica called it—distribution. To men. Every day.

She thought back to that day.

She was so excited to travel by bus to visit their cousins in South Carolina. Sadness still filled their hearts after losing Papa to an accident at work. The employer had given Mama a little money, but Mama would soon need a job. Then the tickets had arrived from their cousins to come for a visit and maybe even stay forever.

She hurried out of the bathroom while Mama washed her hands. She didn't know what possessed her, but she was just so excited and couldn't wait for her mama.

"Olivia, wait for me," her mother called to her.

But Olivia paid no heed and ran out the door, eagerly looking for the bus that would take them to her cousins. She saw a lady who looked a little lost, maybe trying to find her bus. She had nice eyes.

Suddenly, a hand clamped over her mouth, and a strong arm wrapped around her body. She couldn't get a good look at the man, but he carried her away and pushed her in a vehicle.

Olivia blinked and brought herself back to the present. The nightmare seemed like it would never end. Mama must still be frantic. This day held no change. The terrible routine continued, except another man stood with Ricky watching the girls shower. She cringed, feeling the man's eyes on her. Why, oh why, did this happen? Her stomach gurgled with hunger while tying in knots of terror upon fear. The man followed into the room where they ate, and he sat across from her. She kept her head down and ate as slowly as she could, trying to stall the inevitable.

"Enough, Olivia!" Ricky yanked her from the chair. "This man has selected you for a wonderful day." He laughed a deep, cruel laugh. "Here she is. Like I said, hold tight to her, as she might try to run." He bent low so his cigarette smoke-laden breath made her cough. He showed his teeth, still holding remains of breakfast in several spots, and growled. "Be cooperative, or you'll be very sorry."

Ricky shoved her to the man, who dragged her out the door and to his mid-size green car. At least it was clean, but that gave her little comfort. She may never come back. She may not live. Some of the girls said a few had been sent to other countries.

Olivia wiped the tears that traveled down her cheeks with the back of her hand. *Be strong, Olivia.*

She looked around and decided which direction she could run. She pulled on his arm as he focused on unlocking the car door. She wriggled free and started to run. The man cursed, and she heard his footsteps. The footsteps stopped, and she glanced back. He lunged and caught her ankle. She landed hard on the sidewalk, scraping her arm and forehead.

He said nothing but glared with narrow eyes and tight lips. He jerked her to her feet and marched her back to the car. He all but tossed her in and locked her door before sliding into the driver's seat. He swung his right hand and struck her face. "I'll see no more of that behavior. Understand?"

Olivia nodded and then gazed out the window. *Will I ever be free? Will anyone rescue me?*

The car pulled up to a fairly nice hotel. Olivia attempted to quell the shakes that threatened her ability to think.

The man opened her door and once more narrowed his eyes. As they ascended the steps to the front door, he lessened his grip and smiled. "You will smile." It was a command.

She obeyed, though her eyes blinked uncontrollably.

Hector wore his nicest work shirt to work, the one with no stains or tears. He was overdue ordering new work shirts, but he hadn't really thought about it much. He'd never worried about making a good impression with his clothes, only with his work. And he excelled at his work. His wages had increased every six months in the three years he'd worked at the hotel. He always received good evaluations.

He busied himself in the back part of the lounge near the employee entrance. Sofia entered, and he stared.

A slow smile spread across her face. "Morning, Hector."

He nodded. Words wouldn't come. He'd planned all the words, but they stuck in his throat. He coughed.

"You okay, Hector?" Sofia pursed her lips in a sly grin.

"Uh, I was wondering. . . " He pulled his bottom lip between his teeth. He straightened and lifted his chin. "I was wondering . . ."

"What are you wondering, Hector?" Her eyes held laughter. Her eyes were beautiful.

"Um, after work today, could you maybe, perhaps, go to dinner with me? I mean, if you're free . . . of course, only if you'd like to. I'd understand if . . . "

"I'd love to, Hector. And maybe we could go dancing, too."

Hector felt his mouth drop open. *Close your mouth, stupid.* "Why, sure . . . um, that would be great."

"See you after work." Sofia headed to the desk to check in.

When she was out of sight, he plopped in the nearest chair and wiped the sweat off his forehead.

Freddy approached. "Did you ask her? She oozed with happiness when she checked in."

"She did? I . . . yes, I did."

Freddy slapped his shoulder. "Good man."

Freddy glanced up as the man and the girl approached the desk. She had the look of prey. He'd learned to discern the look of the trafficked. It was not that hard to distinguish. The stern man with his hand wrapped around the girl's arm, she with a grimace or head down, fear and pain dwelling in her eyes. And this one sported an ugly scrape on her forehead.

"Good morning, sir. Do you have a reservation?"

"No, just arrived. The other hotel had to cancel due to overbooking."

"I understand. Just give me a few minutes." He plugged in Hector's number and code.

Turning his attention back to the man, he asked, "So, what is the name?"

"Jones. John Jones."

"Very well."

His pager pinged—the code for Hector hung up on a job. Freddy pinged the cleaning ladies. He smiled at the man. "Address?"

The man spouted off an address in another state. Freddy was sure it was fake but dutifully entered the information, asking him to spell the street and the city. Then he sported a sheepish grin on his face and raised a finger to the man. "Just a moment." He picked up the phone. "Ma'am, thank you for holding." He listened and nodded, then grabbed a pen. "Uh huh. Yes, we could do that. It is no problem. We'll send someone to your room shortly. So sorry to keep you waiting." He looked at the man and rolled his eyes, then held his hand over the phone mouthpiece and whispered, "So sorry." He nodded again and spoke into the phone. "Yes. Yes. As I said, we'll be there just as soon as we can." He hung up the phone. "So very sorry. I thank you for your patience. Now, how many nights do you plan to be here, sir?"

"Just one." The man reached for his wallet.

"So will that be credit card?"

"No, cash. How much?"

Freddy named the amount, and the man laid it down. "I hope you have a pleasant stay, young lady." *Good grief, what did I just say?* He felt heat rising up his neck and prayed the man did not see it. The girl looked at him with big, sad eyes. *She's wondering if I have any idea what I'm saying, too.* "That's quite a scrape on your forehead. I have antibiotic if you need it." He looked questioningly at the man.

The man tensed, then laughed. "Bicycle. She wasn't paying attention and tumbled right off." Sternness returned to his face. "She's fine. The key to the room?"

"Oh yes, one moment." Freddy opened the drawer and withdrew the room 802 key. "Here you are, sir. Let me know if you need anything."

The man directed the girl to the elevator.

The elevator doors to the eighth floor opened. The man exited, his grip tight around the girl's arm. He turned in the direction of his room and ran smack into Sofia's cart. He cursed but did not release his ward.

"Sir, I'm so very sorry. Please forgive . . ." She stared at the girl. "Olivia? Is that you?"

The girl's stunned eyes met Sofia's. "The bus station."

The man pushed Olivia behind him. "You are mistaken. Don't you have rooms to clean, woman?"

Sofia shoved the cart into the man, breaking his grip on the girl, and shouted, "Run, Olivia." She grabbed the girl's hand and tore down the hall.

Joanie stepped out of a room. "Here!" Olivia and Sofia scurried into the room, while Joanie shut and locked the door.

Sofia wrapped her arms around the girl as her chest heaved. Olivia seemed frozen. No one said a word, unsure if the man was about to ram the door.

Joanie set her eye to the peephole. She lowered her voice to a whisper. "He's not right out here. But he could be standing just out of sight. Freddy had just pinged me to tell me we had a rescue situation, and then I heard you shout. You know her, Sofia?"

"She's the girl I saw taken at Union Station."

Joanie picked up the room phone. "I'll call Freddy to see what we should do."

Olivia shook and convulsed with silent sobs. Sofia held her close. "Oh, poor child. What terror you've endured. But now, we can return you to your mama."

Oliva stopped and studied Sofia's face. "You know Mama?"

"I talked with her. But the policeman who helped her gave me his card. We'll call him. He'll know how to find her."

The slightest of smiles crossed Olivia's face. Sofia ran her hand through the girl's dark curls. She could feel the grit from the lack of care. Olivia leaned in, perhaps the first loving touch she'd felt since she'd been taken.

"Yes, room 813." Joanie placed the phone on its base. "Freddy saw the man fly out the door and leave in a green car. He recorded a portion of the license number. He's calling the police. Hector is on his way up."

When the knock came on the door, Joanie checked the peephole. "It's Hector." She opened it, and Sofia ran into his arms.

His arms wrapped around her as she shook. "There, there." He patted her back and then addressed the girl. "Young lady, the police are coming." With a gentle smile, he pulled out his handkerchief and wiped Olivia's tears. "When they arrive, they will help you . . ."

"Find my mama." The girl gestured to Sofia. "She saw my mama and has the right policeman's phone number."

"I do." Sofia then related her experience at Union Station. "I need to get my purse, so I can call that policeman.

"Don't leave me." Olivia began to shake again as tears coursed down her face, and she grabbed Sofia's hand.

"We'll all go together." Sofia opened the door and led them to the room where they kept their belongings to retrieve the business card with the officer's phone number.

Several policemen and a policewoman arrived twenty minutes later. They had apprehended the man with the description and the partial license number Freddy had provided. Olivia and Sofia were questioned concerning all that had occurred. Hector brought a sandwich and soda to Olivia.

Forty-five minutes later, a frantic woman ran into the hotel. "Olivia! Olivia!" She hurried to Freddy at the counter. "You have my daughter?"

Olivia stood in the doorway to the breakroom. "Mama? Mama! You're here?" She began to sob and fell to the floor.

Her mother flew to the doorway, dropped to her knees, and wept even louder than her daughter. Then she met Sofia's eyes. "It's you. You found her!" She tore herself from her child and threw her arms around Sofia. "Thank you. Thank you."

Sofia had no words. Tears sloshed down her face as chills ran up and down her spine. How amazing this was to find little Olivia. The reunion wove threads of love and concern for Olivia's future in her heart. What healing needed to be done. What joy they had that Olivia now possessed freedom, at least physically. Emotionally, this sweet girl had a long road ahead of her.

Sofia found her voice. "I'm so happy for you. When the police are done questioning you, you need to get to the counselors that the church nearby makes available to any trafficked family. You have so much healing to be done. You'll need to be very patient."

The policewoman stepped up. "Ma'am, we have apprehended the man who held your daughter. With your permission, we need to question your daughter a little longer and discuss a few things with you. We'll be as brief as possible. You'll be able to accompany your daughter to the hospital to be sure she remains as healthy as possible. The hospital also has counselors, but you are free to search out the counselors you choose. We are familiar with the church mentioned and have worked with them. They are reliable. We recommend that you get your daughter and yourself to counseling as soon as you can. It's truly imperative."

Olivia's mother swallowed hard and nodded.

The policewoman helped Olivia to stand. "We're going to take you and your mom to the hospital in just a few minutes, but we need to ask a few questions now. Is that okay?"

Olivia nodded and walked with her mother and the policewoman into the lounge area. Sofia and the others watched from the doorway of the breakroom as the policewoman asked questions and jotted down notes. Olivia, held tightly by her mother's arms, nodded and spoke softly, swiping tears from her face. Sofia glanced around and saw tears in everyone's eyes.

The policeman who had been at Union Station turned to Sofia. "Ma'am, you and your friends have been a great help." He tipped his hat. "Thank you. The more regular citizens keep their eyes open, the more children we can save." He shook hands with Sofia, Joanie, Hector, and Freddy before leaving.

Sofia gulped. She was not a citizen yet. She would get on that right away. Perhaps Hector would help her.

CHAPTER EIGHT

August 1981

Hector parked his small red Honda Hatchback in front of Sofia and Camila's apartment building. He'd cleaned the vehicle as best he could, getting rid of all food wrappers and soda cans. His mail had covered his back seat but now sat in a box in his kitchen. He'd wiped down the seats with a slightly soapy cloth, enough to clean and freshen but not leave too damp. He drove all the way with the windows down to make sure everything was dry.

Sofia stood at the window and hurried to the door as he approached. She smiled and reached out and ran her hand through his hair. Shivers traveled from her touch to his toes. She giggled. "Hector, did you drive with all the windows down? Your hair is a mess."

Hector grimaced and smoothed his hair. "Yes, I did. I . . . well, I needed to . . . I mean . . ." He contained himself and smiled. "I don't have air conditioning. I hope you don't mind." He held out his arm, and she took it as he escorted her to the car.

The door stuck slightly as he opened it and then made a creaking sound. "This is fine, Hector. I like fresh air."

Hector walked around the back of the car to the driver's side, hoping to calm his rapid heart without Sofia noticing. *Deep breath. Deep breath.*

The dinner club was on a quaint street near the river just below street level. Hector once more held out his arm, and Sofia took it. They maneuvered down the narrow steps and entered a small anteroom that opened to a cozy set of tables arranged next to a small dance floor. The traffic noises and horns honking faded as the sounds of Latino music permeated the dining area.

The host greeted them and led them to a small table in the corner. When Hector let go his nervousness, he found himself laughing and joking with Sofia. She regaled him with stories from her youth, and they discovered they'd grown up about forty miles from each other. She told him of her marriage and divorce and all about Isobel and Manny.

The dinner of empanadas delighted her. "These are the best empanadas. Only my mama could make them better."

"Si, my mama as well. She made everything taste better than anyone else's cooking. I bet your children miss your cooking."

Sofia pursed her lips before allowing a smile to light up her face. "Yes, I'm sure they do. I'm quite sure my ex-husband's sister-in-law is a good cook, but kids want their mama's food. I can't wait to cook for them. I send money, so she can get plenty of food for them. She has other children, so I hope she doesn't mind the extra cooking." Sofia looked down.

Hector laid his hand on hers. "Let's dance."

She nodded and stood. They walked the few steps to the dance floor hand in hand. A few other couples already swayed to the music. Hector placed a hand on her waist and began moving to the beat. Sofia moved effortlessly with him. She fit. He smiled. Never had a girlfriend fit like this. He'd liked a few girls in the past, genuinely cared for them, but this—never a fit like this. She gave him shivers, yet he was so comfortable in her presence. It was jumbled but so clear. A certainty rose in his mind. Sofia was the one.

Sofia. Such a beautiful name. Hector gulped. Thoughts of falling in love assaulted his mind as he drove to her place several days later. Was it too soon? Surely, it was. Still, her beauty enraptured him. But her kindness and bravery called to his heart and left him undone. A life with her brimmed with possibilities. She already had children, and they needed a father. He'd always wanted a big family. Perhaps she didn't. He couldn't ask her yet. He felt red creeping up his neck just considering that prospect. Whatever she wanted—that is, if she wanted him. He shook his head.

He needed to focus on date night. Soon, they would enjoy another dinner out followed by dancing again. She didn't desire fancy restaurants; and for that, he was thankful. A maintenance man did not garner a huge salary, though comfortable. And dancing could be anywhere. He loved her laugh. He didn't even mind when she laughed at his old car.

She wore a simple, colorful dress as she exited her apartment. Her sister stood in the doorway watching her and grinning. Perhaps she knew Sofia held similar feelings toward him. He hoped so. Then he noticed the big basket she carried. He hurried to retrieve it from her.

"What is this?"

She touched his arm, and his skin sparked. "I thought we could do a picnic, since the air is so warm this evening. I'd love to walk along the river. My sister told me there are several parks along the Potomac."

"I know just the one." Still, he stood there, not wanting her to remove her hand.

She giggled. "Hector?"

He cleared his throat and opened the back door, settling the basket on the floor. He then opened the front door and held her arm as she seated herself. Going around to the driver's side, he slid in next to her and put the car into gear, starting down the street toward their destination.

After a fifteen-minute drive and simple conversation about work, he parked the car in a grassy area. There had been no rescues this week, but they all remained alert.

"This park is just north of the airport, and the planes are in landing mode and roar overhead. It's rather exciting; but if you don't like it, we'll go somewhere else."

At that moment, the roar above them brought their eyes to the sky. Sofia gasped and grabbed his arm. "Oh, it's almost like I could touch the plane!"

"Are you okay with this?"

"I love it!" She leaned close and kissed his cheek.

He felt the heat and knew his neck, and probably his face, turned red. He quickly spun around to retrieve the picnic basket and prayed his face would return to normal color.

Hector shook his head. *Focus, man.* He stared at the toolbox. "Just grab the screwdriver and tighten this."

He heard a giggle in the hallway and grimaced. Without a doubt, it was Sara and Joanie rolling their cleaning cart down the corridor. Did everyone know he was smitten with Sofia? Sweet Sofia. He heard smooching noises just outside his door. The teasing never stopped now. He must be in love. Half the time, he couldn't think; and the rest of the time, all he thought about was her. Rippling laughter receded down the hall.

He needed to get his work done. They'd see each other tonight. Sofia was off today; and if he didn't get the work done by five, he'd be here till he got done. He'd skip lunch. If he took the time to eat, the others wouldn't let up needling him about his feelings for Sofia. By skipping lunch, he could make up for the time his mind wandered to beautiful Sofia. He'd promised to pick her up at 6:30.

He picked up his paycheck before leaving work and walked to the bank, open till 6:00 p.m. As he exited the bank, he spotted a jewelry store across the street. It had probably always been there, but he'd never noticed it. Now, it beckoned him. Suppressed thoughts rose. Could he consider it? Would she say yes? He hesitated outside the door. He shouldn't go in. It was just too early. Why did it seem so warm out? Beads of sweat formed on his forehead.

The door opened. The proprietor smiled. "I know how you feel. You're not sure yet. It's okay. Just come in and look around." He held the door open and gestured.

Hector swallowed hard and entered the store.

The owner pointed to a particular glass case. "That's where the engagement rings are, and we do have a sale on a few of them."

Hector shook his head, but the rings called to him. His heart beat faster. They all sparkled with beauty and promise and expense—too much money. He should start saving. Maybe then, he could afford one. He turned to leave, but one little gem caught his eye. He paused and leaned in closer. It was the one, just like Sofia was the one. And the price was not exorbitant. He studied it and checked how he felt inside. Could it be? He blew out the breath he'd been holding and rubbed his chin. He glanced at the salesman.

"It is on sale."

Hector smiled. "I'm a maintenance man. I'm not sure I can afford it."

"Is it the right one, sir?"

Hector closed his eyes and let his shoulders droop. He opened his eyes and studied the ring once more. "I . . . I . . . well, yes, I think it is."

The man removed it from the case and set it before Hector. "Go ahead, pick it up."

If I pick it up, I'll want to take it home. Hector shoved his hands in his pocket. "That's okay. It is perfect, but . . ."

"That's just fine. You should always be sure. And it's on sale till the end of the month."

Hector rubbed the back of his neck. "Thank you." He turned to exit. As his touch landed on the door handle, his legs refused to proceed. The ring was a magnet. It pulled him back. "Wait. Let me look again."

The salesman, about to place the ring in the case, handed it to him.

The thought of this ring on her hand and Sofia forever in his life settled like velvet on him. "I have to get it for her."

"She's a lucky woman. She'll love it. Do you know her size?"

Hector widened his eyes. "Her size?"

"Her ring size. If you can find that out, we can make sure it fits her finger when you propose."

Propose? He was going to propose.

"Or you can take it and then bring her in for us to do the fitting."

"I think her sister might know."

"Good. Let's draw up the papers. We need 10 percent down, 50 percent of the remainder when you bring us the size, and the rest when you pick it up. Will that work?"

Hector stared at the two small diamonds next to the one slightly larger diamond. The white gold setting boasted a filigree design down each side.

"Sir?"

Hector looked up. "She has two small children. I will be their father. It's like the little diamonds are them." He smiled. "And the little vines on the side—that's life—life going on after some difficult times."

"I see you've selected the right one."

"I think it selected me."

"Yes, that happens, sir. Let's get the paperwork done."

The delay of the ring caused Hector to rush to arrive at Sofia's on time. How could he not show his nervousness, his elation, his uncertainty? He'd have to swear Camila to secrecy as to the ring size. What if Sofia said no? He couldn't think about that.

Calm down, man.

Seeing her in the doorway swept all worry from his mind. How was he so lucky to have this beauty waiting happily for him? He kissed her cheek and took her hand, leading her to his car.

They'd decided they loved the parks. So they took turns preparing the food and picking the place. This evening, they were going to Great Falls Park. Hector rejoiced he'd prepared the food the night before. The drive meandered through beautiful, hilly residential areas with large houses and manicured lawns. As they neared the park, with the car windows open, the roar of the falls greeted them. Cheers and hollers rose in a rhythm from onlookers as Hector searched out a parking spot. The breeze wafted sweet with summer blooms. Even in the early evening, the place overflowed with families picnicking, hiking the rocky paths, and standing by the huge boulders separating them from the river.

Hector held the car door for his girl. "I understand they kayak over the falls, and it's pretty exciting to watch. Let's go check out the daredevils before we eat."

Sofia agreed as she climbed out of the car and followed Hector along the path to the falls.

The precarious footing created a slow climb to a viewing area, so Hector gripped Sofia's arm to prevent her from slipping.

As they approached the big rocks and peered over, Sofia gasped and flew into Hector's arms. Her breathing was fast and shallow.

"What is it? Are you okay?"

She panted as she released herself from his hold and took great breaths. "It's just that . . . it took me back to . . ." She paused and looked around. She lowered her voice. "Back to the night I crossed. When I thought I'd drown."

"We can leave. I'm so sorry. I never thought about that."

She placed her hand on his arm. "It's okay. It was only a moment. I just had to catch my breath." She smiled that sweet smile and kissed his cheek. "Let's watch."

The air was fresh. Clouds drifted overhead with the promise of a beautiful sunset. The slight breeze brought relief from the humid air. Hector placed his arm around Sofia's shoulder as they leaned on the nearest boulder to view the kayakers soar over the falls and plunge underwater.

After several seconds, someone nearby gasped. "Should we call 911? They've been under forever. They'll drown."

Then the kayak burst forth from the depths, astounding the viewers. Sofia turned wide eyes to Hector. "How do they do that?"

Hector laughed. "I've no idea. It's a skill I don't have. Let's get our food. I'm hungry."

The picnic tables sat a short distance from the rocks and river. They boasted several families with children laughing and running while parents ate and visited. The antics and happy noises settled in the background of Hector's mind as he gazed at Sofia's face and soaked in her presence. Perhaps he should propose right here while eating chicken legs and potato salad. Should he confess his love first? Would she express devotion back? Should he wait for the ring? Perhaps the longing on her face wasn't for him but for her children as she followed the games and busy behavior around them.

He touched her hand. "They'll be here soon. They will. It'll be okay. You'll be together again."

She smiled. "I know. We'll have to bring them to this park. They'd love it." Her gaze into his eyes almost undid him. Some of that longing was directed his way, yet he perceived some was the pain of missing her children. She looked down. "It just hurts." She tapped her heart. "Right here. I need them. I know they need me."

He stood, desiring to get down on a knee yet knowing she needed an affirmation of her deep heart pain more. As he reached for her hand, a muffled sound caught his attention. He turned as a man walked away from the play area with a little girl. Hector paused. The man had his arm around the child's shoulder, but his other hand covered the little one's mouth. The happy clamor of the picnic area hid any sound of resistance. The man was heading toward the parking area, and the girl was pulling back.

"Sofia! Abduction!" He ran toward the little girl, shouting at the man and tackling him. The abductor let go of the girl as the two men hit the graveled surface of the walkway. The man punched Hector. Blood burst from Hector's nose as he landed his fist in the man's stomach. The man struggled to stand while blackening Hector's eye. Grabbing his ankle, Hector prevented him from escaping. Still, Hector found himself dragged toward the parking lot.

Sofia ran to the little girl. Dozens of adults and children turned. For a moment, stunned silence filled the air. Only the tumult of Hector and the man fighting could be heard. The child clung to Sofia, then wailed.

Sofia yelled, "Help! Help! He's getting away."

As realization dawned, the crowd moved as one toward them. Three men reached the struggle and subdued the kidnapper, while another helped Hector to his feet. By then, park rangers arrived and secured the man's hands behind him.

One ranger turned to Hector. "Please wait, sir, as we'll need a statement from you. Police are on the way."

A woman screamed, "My baby! Sandee! Here I am." She stumbled, as if blinded by tears, to the little girl.

Sofia stepped back as the girl reached for the woman. "Mama, that man tried to take me." The two fell to the ground, embracing each other and weeping.

The woman looked up to Sofia. "Thank you. Thank you. You saved her."

"It wasn't me. It was my . . ." Sofia groaned as she turned to Hector. "Oh, Hector, look at you." She pulled tissues out of her pocket and dabbed at the blood and gravel lodged on his face.

He winced but smiled. "Thank you. The girl?"

"This is her mother," Sofia replied, turning back to the woman standing next to her with the little girl held tightly to her side.

The woman grabbed his hand. "Sir, I understand you saved my Sandee. I can't believe I didn't see him take her. We were all just having so much fun, and the kids were all playing." She wept, and Sofia wrapped her arms around her.

Hector patted her shoulder. "We're just happy we saw it. Actually, I heard it. It must've been God because it was so noisy. We all need to pay closer attention these days."

Sandee walked up to Hector and hung her head. "Mister, thank you." She glanced at her mother, who nodded, then threw her arms around Hector's waist. "I'm sorry he hurt you."

Hector lowered himself to one knee and flinched. "Young lady, you did just what you should have. You hollered, even though he had his hand over your mouth; and you pulled back. Don't worry about me. I'll be fine. I'm so glad you are back with your mama."

Sirens filled the air as three squad cars arrived. Police quickly handcuffed the perpetrator and ducked him into a car. One policewoman came to the mother and Sandee, while another officer approached Hector and Sofia.

"Sir, from the looks of you, you must be the one who stopped the abduction."

Hector nodded. The officer took their statements. As he turned to go, the policewoman joined them and gave Sofia a quizzical look.

"Ma'am, aren't you the one from the hotel who rescued the girl abducted at Union Station?"

Sofia gulped. Would they think she was a part of the kidnappings? Would they send her back? She had her green card, but was that enough? Her answer was a whisper. "Yes."

The policewoman gave her a knowing smile. "We are so pleased to have people like you around. You're aware, and you're saving our children. We need more like you." She glanced at Hector. "Oh my, you two are a team. I didn't recognize you at first with all the blood and the black eye." She chuckled. "Are you all right? Do we need to get you medical help?"

Hector's face was a mess with blood smeared all over it and his nose running, but his eyes sparkled through the purple welts. "I'll be okay. Just a few bruises. We're just happy this girl never went through what Olivia did."

The policewoman reached out and shook Hector's hand. "You two have a good night."

Sofia helped him wipe off his face.

Then as they turned to return to their picnic table, the people who lingered around clapped and called out, "Good job. Thank you."

Sofia smiled. Hector took her hand and nodded. Then he laughed. "Oh no, the squirrels stole our dinner." Their containers of food lay on the ground, while squirrels devoured chicken, potato salad, and chips. "Well, at least we ate some of it."

One of the nearby families called to them. "Come join us. We have plenty. You deserve a feast."

Hector held up a hand, grimacing at every movement. "No, it's okay."

"We insist. Please."

Sofia looked at Hector, then responded. "We'll join you as soon as we rescue our belongings from these squirrels."

The children nearby squealed. "We'll help."

Soon, they sat with the family amid accolades from everyone in the picnic area. Everyone wanted to share food with them. Several had first aid creams that Sofia used on Hector's face after one woman gave her damp cloths to further clean up the blood and dirt. Another had aspirin to help relieve the pain of the bruises.

As the sky darkened, following a glowing display of oranges and pinks, Hector and Sofia slowly made their way to his car.

As Hector started the car, Sofia laid her hand on his and then pulled it to her lips. "Hector, you were so brave. I'm so proud of you."

"I can't imagine—well, I *can* imagine—what would've happened to that little girl. I'm just so thankful that man was stopped."

"You are such a courageous, kind man." She looked down, unsure of herself for a moment, then gave him her sweetest smile. "I . . . I think I might be falling in love with you."

Hector beamed. "I know I am with you."

She leaned over and kissed him on the lips. He winced. "Ouch."

Sofia pulled back. "I'm sorry. You're hurting."

He laughed. "That was the best hurt ever. Can you do it again?"

She gave him the lightest kiss she could. They dissolved in laughter.

Upon arriving at Sofia's apartment, she insisted he come in and get ice for his eye. As soon as Camila saw Hector, she doted on him as much as Sofia. It provided the opportunity to ask her to get Sofia's ring size. Camila squealed. Hector groaned and shook his head as Sofia, who'd gone to the kitchen to get more ice, came running. Camila apologized, telling her she just bumped a bruise on his face. Sofia nodded and returned to get the ice.

Hector lowered his voice. "Call Freddy at the hotel and tell him the size. He'll let me know, and I can go straight to the jeweler from work."

CHAPTER NINE

Freddy looked up as Hector and Sofia walked into the hotel together the next morning. The welts had lessened, but the purple around Hector's eye had brightened. Walking with a slight limp, Hector refused to move slowly and reveal the lingering pain.

"Hector, what happened to you? Sofia, did you beat him up?"

Hector glanced at Sofia, who closed her eyes for a moment, then tilted her head and smiled at Freddy. "No, Freddy, the perpetrator beat him up, but Hector stopped him."

Freddy's mouth dropped open. "No kidding, man? Really? That's incredible, but you look terrible. Do tell."

With a weariness in his voice, Hector related the evening's events.

Sofia's eyes welled up. "That little girl—she'd be gone. It's so terrible. What's wrong with people?"

Hector put his arm around Sofia, while she collected herself. Freddy's eyes widened once more. "Well, now, looks like all this clandestine work has brought you two closer together." He grinned and slapped the counter. "I like it. I like it. I knew . . . "

Hector dropped his arm and frowned at Freddy. "Time to work. See you all later." He turned and went to the maintenance room to fetch his tools. He mumbled to himself all the way. "Now, everyone will know about Sofia and me and tease us relentlessly. Well, they already know."

He paused, looking around, slumping his shoulders. Did anyone hear him? Did he dare propose with a black eye? He couldn't think about that right now. He had to work. He had to ignore the pain and avoid being seen as much as he could. Then he remembered he had to talk to Freddy about the ring.

After replacing a couple sink faucets, Hector returned to the check-in counter. He waited for a couple to finish checking in. "Freddy, I need to tell you something. You can't tell anyone. Promise?"

Freddy grinned. "You mean . . . " He surveyed the hotel lobby and then leaned across the counter. "Camila already called. You are the man! I'm so proud of you. I told you, didn't I? She's perfect."

Hector felt heat crawling up his neck. "Shhh, Freddy. She already called?"

"Yeah, man. Sofia planned to sell her wedding rings from her first marriage." He lowered his gaze. "Sorry if you didn't want me to know she was married before; but she did mention having children, so I kinda figured that."

Hector shook his head. "It's okay."

"So, this morning, Camila took them to a jeweler to get a price and got the size. I thought that was pretty clever. She's really excited."

Hector rubbed the back of his neck. "So, what is it?"

Freddy laughed. "I wrote it down, so I wouldn't forget." He handed over a folded piece of paper. "Proud of you, man."

Stuffing the paper into his pocket, Hector turned to get back to work. He tried to decide if the cold sweat he felt was excitement or nervousness. *I'm really going to do this.* He grinned and glanced back at Freddy, who must've been watching him the whole time. Freddy gave him a thumbs up. Then he noticed a man with a young girl entering the hotel.

Hector wondered if he had great discernment or had just learned to notice the combination of hurt and sullenness that exuded out of trafficked victims. It was all over her face. *Perhaps she's just a stubborn kid.* He threw that thought out and turned toward the man.

The man frowned and narrowed his eyes. "You look like you were in a fight." He feigned a chuckle. "I hope the other guy got the worst of it." He pulled the girl closer and bent to speak to her. "It's okay, honey. We'll check in, and then we'll go get lunch." He looked back at Hector, then turned toward Freddy. "She skipped breakfast and is so hungry." The girl stared at the floor.

Hector took two steps toward the man. He could see Freddy's eyes widen while slightly shaking his head, but he didn't care—the concern for kids in harm's way now overwhelmed all interest in anonymity. He smelled the unkemptness of the man, the sweat evident in his damp underarms. "Yes, I was in a fight. I tackled a man who was trying to kidnap a little girl."

The man stiffened but kept his voice steady. "Oh, I'm glad you're okay. Was . . . did you save the girl?" The girl jerked her head upward toward the man, then looked at Hector with big eyes.

Hector took another step. His pulse pounded in his throat. He fisted his hands. He could see Freddy reaching for the phone. "Yes, the little girl is now safe. It's important that regular people rescue victims of evil men."

The man nodded and cleared his throat. "Well, thank you. Yes, so important. Now, I must get checked in and then get my girl lunch." He took a step away from Hector.

Hector sensed the pleading in the girl's face. She stared at him and mouthed the word *help*. He stepped closer still and gripped the man's shoulder.

The man shoved Hector's hand away. His nostrils flared. "What the devil? Who do you think you are?"

Hector pushed him, breaking his hold on the girl. He heard Sofia's voice behind him, calling the girl to run to her. The man slammed his fist into Hector's chin, then Hector attempted a choke hold but almost got flipped over the other's back.

Freddy hollered. "Police are on the way."

At that, the man disentangled himself from Hector and ran from the hotel. Sofia pulled the girl to a couch and embraced her.

Sirens sounded nearby. Freddy ran to the door. He sighed and hit the wall. "I think he got away. I don't even see his car. Maybe they'll still find him. That was close. Hector, you okay?"

"Yeah, he got my chin and twisted my arm pretty good, but I am okay."

"I'll get some snacks for the girl. Sofia, glad you came when you did." She smiled and turned to the girl. "What's your favorite soda?"

The girl hung her head and whispered, "Cola."

"Can you tell me your name?"

"Katie."

Sofia held her face in her hands. "Well, Katie, we're going to help you get to a safe place and find your family."

Tears dripped down Katie's face. "They won't want me now."

Sofia wrapped her arms around Katie and rocked her. "That is not true. The bad people lied. I can assure you that your family desperately wants you."

Freddy arrived with soda and chips, and Sofia released Katie.

The police soon entered the hotel. It was the same team as before. The officers nodded to Sofia but didn't approach. Sofia opened the snacks and encouraged Katie to eat.

Hector and Freddy detailed the series of events as the officers took notes. While one relayed via radio the information to fellow officers in the area, one cocked his head toward Hector. "Looks like he might have gotten the best of you. Black eye, bruise on the chin. You don't look good."

Hector chuckled and then grimaced as shooting pain found his jaw. "Well, just yesterday, we stopped a kidnapper up at Great Falls. Saved a little girl."

The officer slapped him on the back, causing another wave of pain to traverse his shoulder. "Hey, man, I'm sorry, but that's great. We need more people like you." Then he nodded toward Sofia. "We'll let Officer Delaga talk to the girl. She's good at it."

Hector watched as the officer sat on the couch next to the girl and introduced herself. The child clung to Sofia but answered the officer's questions in a voice barely above a whisper. In a few moments, she returned to where Hector waited with the other officer.

"We're going to take her to the church nearby, where the others have gone. She wants Sofia to go with her, but her shift is about to start, so . . ."

"I'll cover for her." Sara stood by the check-in desk. "I just arrived early to pick up my pay and go to the bank before starting work, but that can wait. I'll start now." She smiled at Sofia and Katie. "Take as long as you need."

Sofia stood, while never breaking her embrace of the girl. "We won't be long. Thank you."

Officer Delaga turned to Sofia. "You can ride with us. We'll finish our questions there."

The other officer shook Hector's hand and then Freddy's. "We sure appreciated your quick response." He turned to Hector. "Better get some ice on that." He poked Hector's arm. "Maybe call us first next time."

Hector finished his workload for the day a half hour after his shift ended. He'd checked out at his usual time and then went back to complete everything. The injuries slowed his pace, and he refused to put that on his employer. He'd just stay till he was done. When done, he reached in his pocket for a few coins for the soda machine and felt the paper. He blanched. He'd forgotten he needed to get to the jeweler before they closed. Sofia was working late, too, but on another floor. She wouldn't see him leave.

They'd planned to walk to the small park nearby, just across from the jeweler, after work. But then everything had happened. Plus, he'd gotten the ring size. He rubbed his face and flexed his shoulders. The initial pains had subsided—nothing sharp but some dull aches still spoke loudly.

He turned around. Freddy studied him. "You okay? Need some time off to recover?"

"No, I'll be fine. I just need to get to the jeweler's and back before Sofia finishes."

"She has an hour left. She and Sara just flip-flopped their shifts. So get going. I'll make up something if she asks about you."

"Thanks." Hector grabbed the soda and headed for the door.

Five minutes later, he withdrew the needed cash from his bank account. He quickly crossed the street to the jeweler's and handed him both the paper with the size and the required payment.

"This is excellent. It's close to the ring's current size. Why don't you wait? Our day slowed down, and we're caught up. We'll finish it right now. It won't take long."

Hector grinned. "Thank you. I'll wait."

The jeweler studied him. "But, oh my friend, are you all right? You're quite banged up. Can I get you some ice? Was it a good fight or an accident . . . that is, if I may ask?"

Hector hesitated. "Yes, a good fight. We, ah, rescued someone from a kidnapping."

"Ahh, this happens much too often these days—a heartbreaking situation. Thank you for helping those caught up in the evil. I knew you were a good man. Sit. We'll get you some ice and have your ring ready shortly." He went to the back of his shop.

His assistant returned with a small bag of ice. Rather than refuse, Hector placed it on his chin and then his shoulder.

The jeweler returned thirty minutes later with the ring in the box all set to go.

Hector studied the ring. It was perfect.

"I have a small velvet bag to put the box in. You go propose to that girl. Do bring her by sometime. I love to meet the couples."

"Thank you, but I can't take it yet. I wanted to see it, but I don't get paid for a few days. I'll need to finish paying for it then."

"Like I said, you are a good man. I trust you. If you are willing to get beat up to rescue others, you'll make your payments. Go. I think this girl is ready to say yes."

Hector looked down and then met the man's eyes and shook his hand. "This is very kind of you. Thank you."

He arrived back at the hotel just as Sofia was checking out.

"Oh, there you are. I thought maybe you'd gone home or over to the church to see how Katie is doing." Her eyes got big, and she grasped his hand. "Can we go over there before our walk, or are you too tired? I'd love to see her, but I can wait if you want."

Hector smiled. This woman delighted his soul. "Yes, let's check on Katie."

They held hands as they walked the short distance to the church. Sofia leaned in. "How do you feel? It must hurt."

"Yeah, it smarts some, but the results were good. I'll heal."

"You're the bravest man I've ever met."

Hector gave her a kiss on her cheek. "You're one courageous woman. I'm glad we're a team."

Sofia's cheeks pinked a bit, and she nodded. "Look, the police car is still there. I hope everything is okay."

As they entered the church, the sounds of sobbing and laughing bounced off the walls. The couple paused. Officer Delaga spotted them and signaled for them to join her. "Katie's parents were contacted and arrived ten minutes ago. What a reunion!"

Sofia wrapped her arms around herself as tears blurred her eyes. "Oh, so soon? That's wonderful."

"Excuse me." The officer walked over to the family and whispered. Everyone turned to Hector and Sofia.

"They saved me, Mama." Katie ran over to Sofia and hugged her.

Sofia got on her knees, so she was eye-level. "I'm so happy your mama and papa are here. I knew they wanted you back. You have some healing to do. They will help you, and so will this church."

The little girl nodded as a tear tracked down her cheek. "Okay. Thank you."

"You are so welcome." Sofia stood as Katie's parents joined them.

Katie's mother fiercely hugged Sofia. "Thank you so much. Our words are not enough, but we are so thankful." The woman's mascara slid down her cheeks along with the tears.

"I'm just glad we were there. You know, she'll have healing to do. It may be difficult at times. This church has people to help."

"Yes, Officer Delaga explained it to us. We'll do anything to help her."

The girl's father pumped Hector's hand. Hector could see the strain and weariness on his face. "You're a brave man. We can't thank you enough. I understand you've done this more than once."

"The children are more than worth it. I'm just sorry they couldn't catch the guy. Didn't even see his car."

Katie's head popped up. "I know what kind of car. It was a white Chevy Nova."

Officer Delaga turned from another conversation. "You know the car?"

Katie smiled shyly. "My papa is a mechanic. He taught me a lot about cars."

Her dad grinned. "It's true. She learned so quickly. I'm proud of you, Katie. Did you get the license plate number?" He turned to the others. "She and I made up games about what the letters and numbers might mean."

Katie dropped her head, apparently concentrating on the memory. "ETG. To me, it meant Every Thing Gone."

Katie's father went to his knees and embraced her. "Oh, honey, thank God not everything is gone. We have you again. Do you remember the numbers?"

"Uh huh—414. It made me think April 14, and I think Easter is around then. That's some hope, Papa."

Katie's mother covered her mouth and shook her head. She whispered. "We thought our Katie was gone, but it's like she was resurrected. It's an Easter for our family."

The officers talked into their radios; and as they ran to the doors, Officer Delaga turned. "Thank you, Katie. You are an amazing young lady."

Hector and Sofia chatted a few minutes and then exchanged phone numbers with Katie's parents. The family then joined the church counselors.

Neither Hector nor Sofia talked as they strolled to the park. Hector felt a heavy peace settle over him. He glanced at her and thought she probably felt it, too. They sat on a bench near the fountain. The fading light from the sun sent sparkles of vibrating colors in the streams of water pulsing into the cooling air of evening. The sounds of the spray and soft splashes dispatched a relaxing effect on them. He placed his arm around Sofia, and she leaned her head against his shoulder.

Hector waited a few minutes, soaking in the wonderful sensations of peace coupled with joy. He put his mouth to her ear. "I love you, Sofia."

With a dreamy expression, she gazed up at him. "I love you, too, Hector."

Hector pursed his lips, then stood. Sofia gave him a confused look. He grinned and pulled the ring box out of his pocket and lowered himself to one knee. Sofia gasped, and her eyes widened.

"Because I love you, Sofia, I never want to be separated from you. I want to be with you for the rest of our lives. Will you marry me?"

Sofia brought both hands to her mouth. A moment later, she pulled them away and clapped. "Oh, yes, yes. Are you sure? My children? Having been married before? Are you sure? I mean, I'm sure, but . . ."

Hector felt his heart swell. "Yes, I am absolutely sure. And because I'm already a citizen, I will go to Bolivia and bring your children—our children—back here just as soon as I can."

Sofia took a deep breath and shook herself. "Really, Hector? You would do that?"

"Yes. Will you give me your hand?" He slipped the ring on her finger. "Notice the two little diamonds? Those are Isobel and Manny."

She held her hand before her face and studied the ring. "You are so kind, Hector, so strong. I don't deserve you."

Hector groaned. "Don't say that. I'm counting on you being happy about this." He chewed his bottom lip.

Sofia burst out laughing. "I'm happy. I couldn't be happier. I love you." She threw her arms around his neck, and they both fell on the ground. They sat up giggling and kissed. "We are going to have a happy marriage. I'm sure of it." Sofia rested her forehead against his and gazed at the ring again.

She sighed. "Hector, I'm going to sell the rings from my first marriage." She studied Hector's face. "I don't know if I told you I still had them."

Hector smiled. "I knew. Camila used them to get your size for this ring. It's fine that you have them."

"Well, I planned to sell them and send the money for the care of the kids until I could go after them. But maybe that money could pay for the flights."

Hector kissed her on the nose. "That sounds perfect, but let's get married soon. That way, I will be Isobel and Manny's father."

Her laugh was rich and infectious. "Yes, they'll have a papa. Also, I'm paying Camila some rent money. Maybe that would be enough to get a bigger apartment for the four of us."

"I'm liking how all this sounds."

CHAPTER TEN

"Hi, Baby." Mama's voice sent soothing beams of warmth through Isobel. "I miss you. Not too much longer."

Isobel's shoulders slumped. "But . . ."

Tía Luisa snatched the phone from her. "Sofia, Sofia. We all miss you. Did we hear there is marriage in your future? I saw Selena at the market yesterday."

"What?" Isobel's voice squeaked, and she grabbed the phone. "Mama, you're getting married? What's his name?"

"Bella, I was about to tell you." Isobel detected a bit of irritation that Tía had told her first. "His name is Hector, and we work together."

"Can we come to your wedding?" Isobel realized her voice was a whine.

"Oh, it'll be a very small ceremony, and we want to save our money. That way, we can get you and Manny and have a good place to live. Sweet girl, can you be patient?"

Isobel nodded, not thinking that her mama couldn't see her. She handed the phone to Manny, even though Tía was reaching for it.

"Mama, when can you come?"

Isobel stepped in front of Tía, so Manny could continue.

"Manny, we'll try to get you as soon as we can. I'm so sorry to make you miss me. I miss you, too—terribly."

Manny let out the sobs that had built up inside.

Tía snatched the phone from him. "He had a cold this week and tends to get dramatic. He'll be fine. I'll give him a couple extra cookies when we hang up. Thank you for calling, Sofia." Tía placed the phone on its holder.

Isobel stood and glared straight into Tía's eyes. "He did not have a cold, and you didn't make cookies. You are a . . ."

The slap missed Isobel because Manny pulled her out of reach. The two ran outside and sat in the dirt in the side yard with their arms around each other.

"Manny, Mama will come. I know she will."

"But what about her new husband? What if he doesn't want us?"

Isobel's breath hitched, and she swallowed hard. "Mama sounded happy and said, 'We'll come get you.' I'm sure she meant it." She pushed away the doubts that now assaulted her. Mama would come. She just had to.

"Bella, I don't want to run away now, no matter how mean Tía is."

She pulled back. "Why not?"

"Mama has to know where we are when she comes. What's his name? Do you think we can call him Papa?"

She patted his back. "His name is Hector, and I think we can call him Papa."

Tía and the cousins marched out of the house and retrieved four paver bricks positioned near the chicken coop.

"Stand up," demanded Tía.

Then the cousins handed two bricks to Manny and two to Isobel.

"For your disrespect, you will hold these bricks over your heads until dinnertime. That is, if you expect dinner."

"Tía, these are heavy." Isobel set them on the ground.

"You heard me. You can stand here all night if you want, without them, or stand here with them over your head until dinner. You will not talk sass to me. Do you understand?"

Isobel nodded and picked the bricks off the ground. She and Manny raised them over their heads as tears trickled down their cheeks.

"Girls, you stay and watch while I finish dinner." Tía Luisa returned to the house, while the cousins sat on the ground and giggled.

Isobel thought of the words from church about forgiveness and Señora Ramos' words to just do what Tía said, but following through was near to impossible. How could she? Her body shook. Anger surged and threatened to explode. Perhaps she'd throw the bricks at her cousins. She glanced at Manny. A pulse throbbed in his neck, and his eyes were pinpoints. Isobel's arms ached. She lowered her arms.

"Mama!" One of the cousins rose.

Isobel quickly raised the bricks again. She would manage. Determination would make her stay until Mama and her new papa came. But never would love be shown to this woman. She might never forgive Tía Luisa. Protection of Manny from this family was paramount.

She whispered. "Manny, give me one of your bricks. I'm bigger than you. I'll hold three."

Manny scowled and shook his head. He stared straight ahead. "I can do it. I'm stronger." He glanced her way. She saw the fury in his eyes.

Two weeks later, Sofia and Hector walked the aisle in the little church near where they worked. Sofia wore a cream-colored knee-length dress that boasted a lacy bodice. The sleeves were three-quarter with a split of four inches and trimmed in lace. Even though she had beautiful dresses that Sofia could have worn, Camila had insisted they go together and find a new dress for the momentous occasion. Camila had paid for the dress as her wedding gift for Sofia. Their shoes were the same size, so Camila gladly loaned her sister a pair of golden sling-back heels. Sofia had managed to bring a necklace belonging to their mother with her to the States and wore that as her only jewelry besides the ring.

Sofia walked down the aisle with Camila arm in arm. Freddy waited with Hector at the front of the church. Chills vibrated along her back with every step closer to Hector. He stood handsome in a suit with a blue print tie. Most of his bruises had faded, and his curly dark hair was trimmed. But it was the love and kindness on his face that filled her heart.

She couldn't have asked for more in coming to this country—the companionship of her sister and a really good job, the friendships at work and this church, plus being able to help young girls caught in terrible situations. But this was the best part—a good man, kind, generous, and brave. His eye still shone with a bit of purple, but those brown eyes overflowed with love for her. If only the children were here, but they would be soon. Hector was already making plans to go after them.

The heartfelt and simple vows buzzed by; and in an instant, she and Hector were husband and wife. The reception was simple as well, hosted by their friends from work. Their gift was a night at a fancy hotel in another section of town.

As everyone greeted them, Freddy spoke in a hushed tone. "All right, you two. No rescues at this place, no heroics, no fights. You be the tourists, the pampered guests. We'll hold down the fort for you."

Sofia laughed as Hector groaned and touched his black eye. "Oh, may it be. Just us."

They spent a delightful evening at the hotel and enjoyed a scrumptious breakfast the following morning. A walk through a park they'd not visited before completed their short honeymoon. All too soon, they returned home to get Sofia moved into Hector's small apartment.

While carrying the few boxes of her things into the apartment, the landlord greeted them. "Hector, I hear you've married. Congratulations. This must be your bride."

Hector shook his hand, then put his arm around Sofia. "Yes, this is my wife, Sofia. And soon, we'll be bringing her two children to join us."

"Well, then, this is fortuitous that I saw you. We have an apartment with three bedrooms coming available. If you're interested, there would be no deposit, since I already have yours."

"How much more is it per month?"

The landlord named the amount. "Think about it. I don't need to know for a few days."

Hector and Sofia exchanged looks. Hector extended his hand again. "We don't need to wait. That price will work. We'll take it."

CHAPTER ELEVEN

The night of the bricks had passed. The ninety minutes might as well have been hours. Tía had given them a paltry dinner instead of the full one the cousins had. The ache in Isobel's shoulders had not left. So at school, she pretended she had no interest in playing ball or climbing on the monkey bars. It hurt too much. Manny did the same. She worried about him as his cheeks looked sunken and his coughing had increased. She'd intended to steal some food at lunch to share at home with Manny, but Señora Ramos always seemed to perceive the need.

Before lunch, she called Isobel to her desk and showed her several items of food. "These will go home with you today. I see that Manny needs extra. Are you able to hide it, so your tía does not notice?"

Isobel nodded. "I think so. Thank you."

"And here is a note inviting you to church again. Do you think she'll let you come?"

"Maybe. It gives them time to do things without us around." She looked down, then raised her eyes and smiled. "We don't mind. We like church. And we don't mind not being with them."

Upon arriving home that afternoon, Isobel gave the bag of food to Manny to put in their secret place near the outdoor toilet. None of the family ever went near the place. While he was occupied, she brought the note to Tía.

The woman scowled. "What did you do now?" She wiped her hands on a towel and opened the note. Isobel thought she growled. "Really? Again? Well, fine. But if I hear one thing about poor behavior by either you or your brother, you'll face the switch. And remember, you get home in time to wash the kitchen floor. Agreed?"

"Yes, Tía." She was about to smile and say thank you but remembered that both grins and scowls brought punishment. She said no more and didn't change her expression.

"Okay, go bring in the laundry and fold it."

"Yes, Tía."

Isobel found Manny in their room eating a banana Señora Ramos had sent. "We have to make sure no one sees that. Climb under your blanket in case the cousins or Tía come in." Manny slipped under the blanket just as one of the cousins entered the room.

"Mama wants you to bring in the laundry. She just told you that. Why's Manny under the blanket?"

Manny threw the blanket back. "Just playing."

"Well, stop. You're here to work. You don't get to play. Mama wants the laundry in now." She smirked and turned, leaving the two alone.

Manny hung his head. Isobel took his hand. "Let's go do the laundry. Tía said we can go to church on Sunday." She lowered her voice. "Where's the banana?"

"In my shirt."

"What? Is it smushed? We'll have to clean it."

Manny laughed. "I ate it all. It's only the peel. I'm going to drop it down the outhouse hole."

Isobel grinned and grabbed his hand. "Good idea. Make sure there's no banana on your hands. We can't get the laundry dirty."

Manny sent his eyebrows up and down. "I could rub the laundry with the peel first."

Isobel chortled, then stopped. "We can't. We want to go to church."

"I know. I know."

Once more, the church service was magical. Isobel didn't know how else to explain it. The music filled her with joy. She'd been happy many times, especially with her mother; but this was different. She didn't understand.

The pastor talked about forgiveness. He said a story found in Matthew, chapter eighteen, told about a man who owed the king a lot of money. The king was going to put him in jail, but the man begged for forgiveness and said he'd pay it all. The king told him he was free to go and didn't have to pay him.

Isobel shook her head. What a surprising thought. She'd heard Tía Luisa and her husband talk about people that owed them money. They would never let them off the hook. This was some king.

The pastor continued. "The forgiven man went out and cornered another man, who owed him just a little bit; and he threatened to throw him jail. When that man begged, the first man put him in jail, anyway."

Isobel could see Tía being like that.

The pastor spread his arms out and grimaced. "Well, people went and told the king, who sent for that first man, called him wicked, and threw him in prison, too. The king did this because that man didn't forgive after he'd been forgiven. Jail in those days was a place of torment."

I must be in jail. Tía Luisa torments Manny and me all the time.

The pastor said that when people don't forgive, they get tormented. It was confusing. Isobel struggled to make sense of it. Perhaps Señora Ramos could explain it more. Did that mean she should forgive Tía for the bricks? That couldn't be it. The tormenting that cascaded over Manny and her originated with Tía, not with her.

Then the pastor made a statement. "John 3:16 tells us that God so loved us that He gave His son to die for us. If we believe in Him and ask, He forgives us of every sin. If we allow His love to be in us, we can forgive everyone who sins against us. That's true freedom."

A stunned feeling overtook Isobel. She'd sworn she'd never forgive Tía that night of the bricks. It was wrong—so wrong. It was unfair. No one should do that to anyone. Tía should be in jail. Isobel assured herself that forgiveness probably didn't apply to her situation. Sure, there might be worse situations, but still . . . However, she would think about it. She liked God's love. What she knew of it felt really good—and real. But extending that to Tía Luisa? She just wasn't sure.

"Are you okay, Bella?"

Isobel looked up. Manny stood next to her, and most of the people had left. "Oh, yes, I'm fine. Just thinking."

"Señora Ramos is waiting by the door."

Isobel hopped off the pew and hurried to the entrance with Manny.

"There you are. Will you stay for the picnic?"

Isobel nodded. She'd decided they would eat plenty and take extra home. Manny needed the strength that only food seemed to give. "Yes, Señora. We thank you for this."

Señora took her hand and Manny's and went directly to the food line. "Take as much as you want."

Marriage was wonderful. The limp had disappeared, and now Hector felt like skipping. Childish? Probably, but he couldn't be happier. The plane tickets were purchased. Soon, he'd bring Sofia's children back to her. No—they were his children, also, and he would love them as his own.

He looked up. Freddy had his perpetual grin. "Told ya, Hector. So happy for you two. Hope I can be as lucky."

"Me, too. Don't try to impress the girls with your car. Just be the good guy you are."

Hector picked up the list of repairs needed for the week and turned toward the maintenance room. Freddy cleared his throat.

Hector turned. A man approached the check-in desk with a teen girl in tow. The girl was grumbling and rolling her eyes. The man looked exasperated. Hector pretended he was studying his list and waited.

The man looked apologetically at Freddy. "Sorry. Teens." He bent close to the girl and lowered his voice. "The decision is made. This is what we're doing."

The girl stiffened, and the man grabbed her arm. "Don't."

Freddy smiled and reached for his pager. "Checking in? Name?" He raised his eyebrows at Hector, who stuffed the list in his pocket and set his stance.

Just then, a woman with twin boys burst into the hotel lobby. "I promised the boys pizza for lunch. What a crazy day." She glanced at the teen girl. "Maddie, you're not still mad, are you? We can get to that movie tomorrow. It's nice today, and we're going to the museums. It's decided."

She glanced around and saw Hector and then turned to the man with the girl. "Are we creating a scene, Bob?" Then she addressed Freddy. "So sorry, sir. We're a little off. The plane was late, and then the cab got lost."

Maddie shook her head. "Mom, you gave him the wrong address." She rolled her eyes again.

Freddy chuckled. "It's so nice to have you here. Let's get you checked in, so you can be on your way to lunch and the museums. We do have shuttles if you don't want to take a cab. The brochures are right there." He nodded at Hector.

Hector sighed, hoping the family didn't hear him. He was so glad he didn't have to slug some man who really was a family man with a typical teen daughter. He wished he could tell Maddie how lucky she was to have a normal life. He looked up, and Sofia stood in the doorway of the breakroom. Sofia raised her eyebrows in question.

Hector joined her and explained how they had almost paged her, mistaking a normal family for another abduction. Sofia peeked out at them as they checked in. The boys punched each other and ran into the lounge with the mother trying to corral them. The teen girl continued rolling her eyes and shaking her head. The dad kept apologizing to Freddy, who just smiled.

Sofie took Hector's hand. "You know, our children may well act like that. They're good kids but certainly not perfect."

Hector laughed. "We'll manage."

She looked down. "I miss them so much."

"Only a week or so and they'll be here." He gave a quick kiss to her cheek. "I have to get to work. See you later."

CHAPTER TWELVE

October 1981

Hector felt the creases of weariness etched in his face. The flights and all the traveling to Luisa and Victor's home were exhausting. When he called to tell Luisa he would be there the next day, she wanted him to wait. He refused; and then, upon arriving, he saw why. Selena had told Sofia and him what they might see. Without asking, he barged into the area where the children slept. The drafty room looked as though they'd tried to dress it up quickly. They hadn't succeeded. One look at the children, and it was obvious the money sent for their care didn't provide food for them. They were too thin, almost like trafficked kids. He loved them the moment he met them. He found Luisa difficult and rejoiced to remove the children from her care. He only stayed an hour, and then they were on their way home.

The children were handling it better than he thought they would. Somehow, by the grace of God, they trusted him. Thankfully, he'd been able to call Sofia, so she could soothe their fears. Still, it'd been a year since they'd seen their mother, and he could see the sadness they carried. Isobel cared for Manny like a little mama. Determination to protect him was fierce in her eyes. Manny had a strong spirit, but he was so physically weak now and anemic.

The bus they rode in to the airport sported dirty and torn seats. Still, they were able to stretch out on the seats for part of the three-hour ride. Mostly, Manny and Isobel sat huddled next to Hector.

"Your mama can't wait to see you. Are you hungry?"

They both nodded. Luisa had not offered any food for them to take along; but Isobel directed him to the market, where he purchased cheese and fruit.

Manny said nothing until an hour into the trip. "Are you really going to be our papa? You married Mama? Are you sure you're not stealing us?"

Isobel interrupted. "We had friends at school who were stolen; and Cousin Selena said if we ran away, we might be stolen."

Hector shook his head. "You were thinking of running away?"

Manny narrowed his eyes. "Tía Luisa was so mean. Are you sure we don't ever have to see her again—that we'll be with Mama? Are you sure?"

"I'm sure, Manny. Your mama misses you so much."

Hector approached the immigration official. Once he stamped the papers, they would board the plane and soon reunite with Sofia.

The official regarded him with suspicion. His gaze bored through Hector and then Isobel. Finally, he studied Manny. "He is too sickly, señor. I cannot allow him."

The gasp from Hector surged out of him, and his shoulders slumped. "No, sir, I must take him. I've come all this way."

"And what is he to you? He will not glean much money for you. Look at him."

Hector felt his eyes bulge. He tightened his grip on the children's hands. The room seemed foggier, the lingering smell, sweaty. "What are you saying, man?"

The laugh was gruff. "Do not pretend I don't know what happens to many. I see much. I know much. I say little."

Hector laid his hand on the boy's shoulder and tugged him against his side. He glared at the official. "This boy is my wife's son, her own flesh and blood. I'll not leave him behind."

The man nodded. "I understand. Please forgive my presumption. So, to expedite this unlikely approval for travel . . . " The words hung in the air. The man tilted his head.

Hector squinted. "So . . . " He pressed his lips together as understanding dawned. He glanced around as he felt his palms exude sweat. "What is your price to stamp his papers?"

The official bent near and brought his hand to his mouth. He coughed. A whisper then emerged from behind his hand. "Two hundred will do."

"Bella, hold Manny's hand." Hector groped his pocket and pulled out his wallet. As he fished out the money, he felt, more than heard, footsteps behind him. Feeling guilt all over his face, he looked at the official.

"No worries, he is not the police. He is what I thought you were."

This time, a flush of anger crept up Hector's neck. The official locked eyes with him and gave the slightest shake of his head. Hector took a deep breath and handed the money to him.

The official looked at the man who'd approached. "Sergio, I have a deal for you. This man will take your girl for you. He'll give you three hundred. Save your airfare."

"And why would I agree to that?" Sergio's voice held a snarl.

"Look. The two girls can help each other. And the boy won't bring much. He's sickly."

Hector glanced at the man. He held a girl whose face wore pain and fear. The man shrugged his shoulders. "For another hundred, I can dispose of the boy if you like. You have four hundred?"

The official slid the two hundred back across the table to Hector and raised his eyebrows. "Give him three hundred for the girl. You'll be reimbursed when you sell them, maybe even get more since you have two girls."

No words came. Wallet still in hand, Hector withdrew another hundred and gave the three hundred dollars to Sergio.

"You're keeping the boy?"

Hector nodded.

He shoved the girl to him and walked away.

The official smiled. "You've just added to your family. This girl would've been sold for sex."

"I gathered that."

"You do need to pay her airfare."

Hector nodded and doled out the necessary funds.

"Now she'll have a home. As I said, I see much. I see you are one who will keep his family safe. Young lady, what is your name, so I can put you on the plane? You now have new parents, a sister, and a brother."

The girl shook and looked at the floor. "Gabriella."

"But what about her family?" Hector turned to the girl. "Were you stolen?"

Bella reached over and took her hand. "It's okay. We want to help."

The girl didn't smile or cry. She stared straight ahead. "I ran away. My mama died, so my papa drank all the time. He beat me, so I left. That man fed me and then brought me here."

Bella leaned close. "I almost ran away, too. But now my new papa came, and we are going to be with him and Mama. I'm Isobel, but I go by Bella. And my brother is Manny."

Everyone jumped as the official stamped four documents to gain them access to the plane. "You go now. Have a good life. Today, I feel even my life is a little better. I will sleep good tonight." He smiled at Hector. "You're welcome. So go. Now."

The small group boarded the airplane destined for Washington, D.C. Bella gripped the armrest of her aisle seat with one hand. Her other hand held Manny's. Gabriella sat next to the window and stared out at the moving scenery. The roar of the engines engulfed Bella. She didn't know if she should cover her ears or climb under the seat. The plane's speed increased. Bella closed her eyes. The surge of lift-off took her breath away. Prying her eyes open, she looked at Gabriella, who started to laugh. Soon, they all giggled. They were in the air, on the way to Mama. Excitement, nervousness, and weariness rushed through her.

They all slept off and on as exhaustion overtook them. Isobel refused to release Manny's hand. Her conviction to protect him overwhelmed her. She liked Hector, her new papa, but remained wary of almost any adult. She'd trusted Señora Ramos, who was kind. Most of her teachers and the people at church seemed good, but Tía Luisa had drained her of so much trust.

Hector smiled at her across the aisle. "They're going to bring you some food soon. I'll wake you up if you fall asleep."

He had a nice smile. He'd been willing to pay extra for Manny and refused to leave him behind. She'd decided then she could depend on him. And he'd paid for Gabriella, rescued her from that awful man. Hector was a good man.

"Thank you, Mr. . . . um, Hector. Should we call you, umm . . ."

Hector reached out and patted her shoulder. "Isobel, I married your mama. As far as I'm concerned, that makes you my daughter. You can call me Papa if you like. I would love that. But if it's too soon, you can call me Hector."

Warmth ran through her. "I'd like to call you Papa; and you can call me Bella, if you like."

Manny leaned out. "I like you, Papa. Thank you for coming after us. We didn't like Tía Luisa."

Papa smiled. "I understand."

Gabriela peeked around Manny and Bella. "May I call you Papa, too? I don't have any other family." A tear tracked down her cheek. "And you can call me Gabi."

"Gabi, I will now be your papa, too."

Gabi's countenance lifted, and a smile spread across her face and shone through her eyes.

Manny took Gabi's hand. "I have two sisters now." He turned wide eyes to Isobel. "Is that okay, Bella?"

She squeezed her brother's hand. "Yes, Gabi is our sister now." She swung her head to Papa. "What will Mama think about having another daughter?"

Papa shook his head and rubbed his chin. "She'll probably be quite surprised, but I know she'll be delighted. We have an apartment with three small bedrooms. So the girls will share a room, and Manny will have his own. Is that okay?"

Gabi spoke first. "I'll sleep wherever you want me to."

Manny and Isobel studied each other. Manny straightened his shoulders. "We've always had the same bedroom and sometimes slept with each other to keep warm. Tía Luisa punished us for that. But Señora Ramos explained that boys usually have their own room and girls have theirs and that it's important as you grow older. I think that will be okay. Bella?"

She nodded and scrunched her shoulders. "I know. Yes, yes, we should." She grimaced. "It might be a little hard at first."

Hector reached over to take her hand. "You'll all be safe and warm and well-fed. And you'll be together most of the time."

The food arrived then, and everyone gave their attention to eating.

The lay-over in Bogota was only ninety minutes. Weariness sat on each of them, but the children stayed close to Hector. He sighed in relief that the girls could accompany each other into the restroom while he accompanied Manny. The girls listened with big eyes to all his warnings to not even talk to anyone. They were able to get some snacks and more cheese before the six-hour flight home. The children were asleep before the plane lifted high into the air.

CHAPTER THIRTEEN

Sofia and Camila stood together at the gate and watched the plane land. Hector had sent a telegram informing them of the arrival time.

Squeezing her sister's hand, Sofia swiped her eyes. "I can't wait. My babies. But, oh . . ." She let go of Camila and gripped her stomach as she bent over. "Will they hate me for leaving them this long?"

Camila placed her arm across Sofia's shoulders. "Chin up, girl. Your babies love you and have missed you mightily. It's been rough on them, according to Selena. They may be hesitant. They may need some emotional healing. But most of all, they need you. Didn't you say your hotel is giving you a few days off?"

"Yes, everyone was so kind. The other cleaning girls promised to cover for me as long as I need. The big boss had a long talk with Hector and gave him time to go get them and then came and told me to take as long as I need."

"Sofia, wipe your eyes. Passengers are disembarking."

"I'll just cry more when I see them."

Sofia held her breath and wrapped her arms around herself. "Is that . . . oh, not them. This is the right plane, isn't it?"

Camila looked at the reading on the nearby screen. "It's the right one. They'll be here. Oh, oh, is that them?"

Isobel and Manny emerged from the tunnel with Hector right behind them. The children looked every direction, seemingly frantic.

"Babies!" Sofia wasn't sure if she screamed or not. She didn't care. The children locked their eyes on her and ran. She dropped to her knees and opened her arms. The feeling of them in her arms caused every fear and worry to flee. She had her babies.

Isobel sobbed, and Manny grinned as tears flowed freely out of his eyes. She didn't want to loosen her embrace, but she had to study their faces. How they'd grown. Bella, a young woman almost, probably had to grow too fast, taking care of Manny. And, oh, how he'd grown—still a little boy but wanting to be tough and strong.

She took each face in her hands and kissed them so many times. They laughed and cried. When she finally stood, they each pressed in to her side. So good to feel them next to her. Never would she let them be apart from her again. She would plead their forgiveness, but now they would celebrate and rest.

Hector stood in front of her, smiling. "They are finally here; and yes, they are my children, too."

"My darling, thank you for retrieving them, for rescuing them." She hugged her man with her two children wrapping their arms around their new papa as well.

Hector stepped back too soon. Sofia searched his eyes. He reached behind himself and took the hand of a young girl about Bella's age.

"Mi Amor, this is Gabriella. We call her Gabi. We rescued her as well." He pierced Sofia's eyes with his look. "And yes, I mean *rescue*."

Sofia flashed comprehension of what he meant.

"And she is now our daughter, as well. Gabi, this is your new mama."

Sofia looked with a moment of questioning to Hector. Then she smiled, swallowed, and moved forward, taking Gabi in her arms. "Young lady, Gabi, I am so glad you are here, and our home is now your home."

Gabi tentatively wrapped her arms around Sofia and then sobbed as Sofia's embrace tightened around her. When the sobs lessened, Sofia took a tissue and wiped her eyes. "Now, now, Gabi, let's go home with our family."

Conversations would ensue. Her family would settle in. All would be revealed and discussed, and healing would take place. Confidence rose that forgiveness would be given. They had much to look forward to.

Bella loved Gabi. It was hard to let Manny be in a different room, but Mama had decorated his room with boy things—footballs, soccer balls, cars, lions. And her room with Gabi was full of lacy covers, dolls, lambs, bunnies, and lots of pink. She knew it was right. A few nights in that first month, Manny came into her room and crawled in with her. No one minded, and that made her happy. Gabi was provided an extra bed from the hotel. As soon as they heard the harrowing story of her rescue and knew what almost became of her, they found the bed and took a collection to get her bedding and some clothes.

Mama told Bella of the girls they tried to rescue, the ones they lost, the ones they rescued, and the story of Olivia, who now regularly attended the church that helped so many. It was the church where Mama and Papa belonged, and the children went with them. It reminded Bella of Señora Ramos' church, and she liked it.

One day, Bella poured out the wounds Tía Luisa had inflicted on her heart. How hard it was to forgive. She knew Mama was mad at Tía as well, but Papa reminded them of forgiveness. Mama would nod, and Bella would hang her head. She had almost promised herself to never forgive Tía, so she gasped out the night of the bricks and the promises she'd made. Mama cried and begged her forgiveness for leaving her there to endure such treatment.

"Mama, I forgive you. I've never hated you. I love you, Mama, but I do hate Tía Luisa. And even though Señora Ramos told me to forgive and just put up with things and do what she asked, after the bricks, I decided to maybe never forgive her. I mean, wasn't it wrong? Wasn't it hateful what she did to us? All those things, all that meanness?"

Mama held her close and spoke into her hair. "It was wrong. Very wrong. I'm so very sorry you had to be there. Thank you for forgiving me."

Bella pulled back. "But do we have to forgive her? The pastor said there is torment when we don't forgive. Is that true? He told a story from the Bible about a king that let a man go free who owed him a really big bunch of money. And then that man threw another man in jail who just owed him a few dollars. When the king heard about it, he threw that first man in jail. The pastor said he would be tormented there and if we don't forgive, we'll be tormented. But Tía Luisa tormented me and Manny."

Mama gazed into the distance and sighed. "I've heard that story at church. And the kids we've rescued are taught to forgive in order to be free. When you forgive, it sets you free."

"But Tía Luisa was wrong."

Mama took her hand, pulled it to her lips, and kissed it. "She was wrong. Maybe she will ask you for forgiveness one day. We hope she turns to God. But if you forgive her, it sets you free from the anger and hurt that you feel from all she did."

"It's hard, Mama. She was terrible to us. I don't want to forgive, but I guess I could think about it."

Manny walked into the room. "I won't forgive her. If I ever see her again, I'll punch her in the face."

Mama pulled Manny into her arms. "I'm so sorry this happened, Manny. Can you forgive me for leaving you there?"

Manny straightened. "It wasn't your fault, Mama. It was Tía Luisa. She was mean."

Gabi had entered the room behind Manny. "My mama taught me to pray; and when she was sick, she was afraid what would happen to me 'cause Papa already drank too much and was sometimes mean to her. She taught me about forgiveness. She said she'd forgiven Papa when he'd hurt her and made me promise to forgive him, even if he hurt me after she died. She also told me it was okay for me to leave, but she didn't know where I could go for help."

"Did you forgive him?" Manny took Bella's hand.

"I didn't want to, but I could always hear her voice in my head. So eventually, I did. And then I left."

"But then that terrible man found you."

"And he fed me. I thought he was nice, at first. But I began to realize what he was going to do with me. I almost ran away again; but he stopped me and brought me to the airport, where you bought me."

"Oh, no, no!" Mama stood and hugged Gabi. "We didn't buy you. We just gave the man the money, so he'd think we did. You're our daughter now and not our property. We love you, Gabi. Your mama was a very wise and kind woman. I'm sorry your papa was not kind. I think we all need to think about forgiveness. We're going to heal better if we can forgive. Can each of you promise me you'll really think about it?"

Bella raised her head. "Mama, can you forgive Tía Luisa like Gabi's mama forgave her papa?"

"I don't think I've fully done it yet, but I want to. I want us all to forgive. Our family will be stronger, and we'll be able to rescue more girls if our hearts are free."

"Well, at least she can't hurt us anymore. And I won't let anyone hurt Manny ever again."

Manny faced his sister. "I can take of myself, but I will protect you."

CHAPTER FOURTEEN

NOVEMBER 1981

Manny burst through the door.

Bella gasped and rushed to him. "Manny, what happened?"

Blood dripped across his forehead, and his eye boasted black and shiny. "I don't like the boys here. And they don't like me." He brushed his sister's hand away as she attempted to wipe his forehead with the dish towel already in her hand.

"But . . ."

Manny stomped his foot. "Stop, Bella. I don't care what they think."

"But those boys are bigger than you."

"I'm tougher, and they know it." He snatched the towel from her and wiped his face, which just smeared the blood everywhere. He winced when he rubbed it over his eye.

"Manny." Bella turned to see her mother with a sad but kind expression. "Come here, boy."

Manny stood still and shook his head. "I'm fine." His voice lowered, and it held a quiver. "I don't like it here."

Mama dampened another cloth in the dishwater and walked over. Without a word, she dabbed at Manny's face with gentleness, cleaning up the blood. She turned to Bella. "Fetch me some ice and wrap it in another cloth."

When Bella handed it to her, she sat down and pulled Manny onto her lap. He wriggled out of her grasp, but she pulled him back and returned him to her lap. "Where do you think this toughness came from, young man? I was tough long before you. We need to be tough to survive this life." She placed the ice on his eye. He flinched but allowed his mama to hold it there.

Bella dragged a chair next to her mama and sat down.

Mama patted her hand and then focused again on her brother. She lowered the ice and set it aside. She lifted his chin so his eyes were even with hers, but he looked away.

"Manny, I've heard their taunts. I know you're tough. I'm not going to punish you for fighting. You're strong—you're really strong—and you can beat them up."

Manny sighed, and his shoulders loosened. "I can? It's okay? 'Cause I'm just as good as they are. I don't care what they say. I can beat them all up." He looked straight at Mama. "I like winning. I like fighting."

Mama's laugh sounded strangled. She looked down and shook her head. "No, my boy. No, it's not okay. I understand. I'm tough, too, and I want to beat up anybody who's mean toward you or your sister or Gabi. But, Manny, we can't live this way. You are a tough warrior. I saw it in you when you were a baby. But use it to get along, to do well in school. Be smart, Manny."

Bella glanced up as Papa walked into the kitchen. He surveyed the scene. "Manny, I hope you landed the biggest blow. Some of those boys out there are nothing but trouble. But we don't want you to be considered trouble. Like your mama said, you are a warrior—a triumphant warrior—but you must pick your battles. Battles in the neighborhood are not worth the problems they create. I want you to be smart. Use your toughness to outsmart them."

Manny slipped off his mama's lap. "You don't get it, Papa. They want to fight. They want to taunt and mock anyone who's new. They think I'm worth nothing. I'd rather go after them before they sneak up on me."

Papa cleared his throat. He tilted his head toward Mama, and she nodded. "Manny, we don't want to cause trouble that comes to the notice of the police. Your mama has not yet obtained her citizenship, and we don't want to bring attention to that. The police like the rescue work we do, but we don't want to be considered troublemakers around here."

Bella gasped. "What? Could they . . . Mama, would they send you back?" Tears welled in her eyes.

Mama pulled Bella to her chest. "I don't think so, but we're not sure. So we don't want to cause trouble. We're already angering the people who hurt little girls like Gabi. We just don't want to have unrest in the neighborhood."

"Do some of those men live in our neighborhood?"

"We don't know, so keep your eyes open. Be safe." She turned to Manny. "We need you to help protect your sisters and notice what's going on in the neighborhood, not starting fights." She smiled and looked to Papa. "Maybe Manny could beat up some of those men. He's probably strong enough."

"Mama! No! You don't mean that, do you?" Bella swiveled her head toward her mama, papa, and brother.

"No, Bella. We don't want that."

Manny jutted out his chin. "I could do it, though. I wanted to beat up Tía Luisa, but she's a girl."

Papa shook his head and ran his hand through his hair. "No, no fights. Manny, we don't want you to back down from these boys, but we don't want you going after them, either. Can you do that?"

Manny grimaced and looked down.

Mama reached out and took his hand. "Manny?"

The boy pulled his hand away and ran out the door.

Papa sighed. "I don't know. Do you think he heard us?"

Mama gazed upward. "I don't know, Hector. I don't know."

School would start soon, the thought assaulting Bella with glee and terror. The other kids at church assured her it would be fine, but the memories of treatment from Tía Luisa and some at school in Bolivia continued to threaten her. What if these students made fun of her just because she was new? What if lunch wasn't enough food? What if she missed days and got behind? Mama reminded her that none of that would happen now, and Bella attempted to trust that implicitly. She missed fun lessons in math and reading and hoped she could catch up. Mama and Papa had made them wait a while before starting, claiming it gave them time to become a family again.

She thought how Manny had already fought with the neighborhood kids. Mama had explained to her that as the newest boy, he was the least accepted and attempted to prove his worthiness with his fists. For a small boy, which brought taunts, his strength matched the biggest of boys. Mama said he embraced this new persona and sought out those who would taunt or challenge him. It was a triumphant march for him, and no amount of caution from the family had slowed his march. She also said Papa found his warnings ignored and worried the anger from Manny's time in Bolivia would land him in serious trouble.

A few mornings after the family discussion, Gabi tilted her face and then looked down her nose at her new brother while they ate breakfast. "Manny, you remind me of my papa."

Manny smirked. "You think I look old."

"No, you look mean like he did. Do you want to be an old drunk who beats on people?"

Manny's eyes looked everywhere but at Gabi. "Why would I do that?"

"Your tía was mean. My papa was mean. It was wrong. Right?"

"Yeah, it was. Really wrong."

"So, you want to be mean?" Gabi leaned forward and placed her hand on his.

Manny jerked his hand away and narrowed his eyes. "Not mean like them. But the boys around here are mean, and they shouldn't be that way, just like Tía and your papa shouldn't have been that way."

Bella allowed her eyes to widen but put her hand over her mouth. The realization was stunning. Could Manny turn out just like what he hated?

Gabi continued her stare at Manny. "I'm afraid you'll be like my papa."

Manny pushed his cereal bowl away and stalked out of the house.

Bella looked at Gabi and shook her head. They finished breakfast in silence.

The pastor stood to preach. Bella and Gabi, adorned in the new dresses Tía Camila had purchased for them, placed their hands in their laps. Yellow with white lace trim delighted Bella, while Gabi thrilled in her light blue with pleats. Manny, smartly dressed in a tan shirt and dark blue pants, sat between the girls. Gabi, age eight, fit perfectly in this family, filling the gap between Bella, age nine, and Manny, age seven. Her long dark hair made her look so much like Bella that some even thought they were twins.

"The Bible tells us in Galatians 6:7 that we will reap what we sow. That means that what we plant is what will grow. If we plant or sow seeds and acts of kindness, we'll find that kindness grows around us. If we sow seeds of anger, we'll find angry situations at every corner."

Gabi nudged Manny. He threw a pointed look at her and fisted his hands in his lap.

"Now, we all have capabilities to choose the seeds we plant. It might be hard because others have sent bad seeds into our lives by their actions. At this church, we deal with people who have had abuse and terrible times at the hands of others. It can be a hard recovery. But now, we make choices as we allow God's love to change and heal us. If we want revenge—and that can be a strong desire—it will only bring more pain.

"In Romans 12, God says that vengeance is His to do. Wow! He knows what happened to you and who did it. He can take care of them, change them, repay them if needed. And you know, we work closely with law enforcement to put an end to abusive behavior. But think how He rescued you. Maybe you're angry or hurt that you weren't rescued sooner, but you *were* rescued. We all have a lot of baggage—bad memories and experiences that still yell in our minds and that we need to leave with Jesus. He can handle it. We cannot.

"It's why He rescued you. Think about the story of the Good Shepherd. You were the one caught in the thorns and on the ledge of the cliff. None of us wanted to be that one, but we were. Did the Good Shepherd say, 'Well, too bad, that's a tough break. I suppose I'll lose a few'? Nope, those words aren't in His vocabulary. Instead, He leaves the ninety-nine in a safe place and goes to find that one. He takes His staff to fight off the bad animals that would bring injury and His shepherd's hook to grab his little lamb and pull him off the ledge. And when He finds that lamb, He raises the little one to His shoulders and carries it home with great rejoicing. The Bible is full of stories of how God rescues us.

"In John 10, He says He wants us to have abundant life. The devil seeks to destroy us. God has rescued so many from destruction. We must move forward and allow Him to restore abundant life to us. It's a choice to give up our angry responses and let them be replaced with God's love and forgiveness. Please know this church is dedicated to help anyone and everyone who's been hurt find their way to fullness of joy and life."

Manny hung his head. Bella took his hand, which no longer sat in a fist. She didn't look at him. She would wait. He would have to think through this, but it seemed like a map had been laid before them. It was the path they all needed to take. She hoped Manny would choose to walk that path with her.

She lowered her head as the pastor prayed and whispered, "God, I promised to never forgive Tía Luisa, but You rescued me. I thought Señora Ramos and my new papa rescued me, but I see now it was You. I want to forgive. I want to break that promise I made and forgive. Will You help me? I'm sad she hated us, but I'm sorry we hated her. Please forgive us and help us live like You want us to. Amen."

Bella looked up, but everything was blurry. Then she realized her eyes were full of tears. She wiped them with the back of her hand. Manny nudged her. When she glanced his way, he nodded and gave her the slightest of smiles. She hugged him. Little smiles seemed like bubbles inside, floating all through her. She wanted to giggle. Maybe that was the joy the pastor had talked about.

CHAPTER FIFTEEN

SEPTEMBER 1983

Cousin Selena called. Tía Luisa and her family were moving to the States. Isobel shook her head and walked outside. Mama followed, carrying Liliana, born a year before, and joined Bella on a bench.

"Bella, I do hope they don't move close to us; but if they do, are you okay with that? I personally want to slap her face. She deserves much worse for what she did, but I've come to understand that I can't live with that anger in me." She wrapped one arm around her daughter, while holding Liliana on her lap with her other arm.

Bella pursed her lips and gazed everywhere except at Mama. She shook her head. "I think I've forgiven her, but my stomach hurts just thinking about seeing any of them again." She buried her head in Mama's shoulder and cried. Liliana patted her face, and she took her baby sister in her arms.

"We won't let them come to visit, then. And we certainly don't need to go to see them."

Straightening her back, Bella shook her head. "It's been two years. I'm doing good in school. I have friends. I've forgiven her. She can't hurt me anymore. Even if she tried, you and Papa wouldn't let her. I suppose she could hurt my feelings, but then, so could anyone."

"If she does, I really will punch her."

Bella jumped. "Manny, you scared me." She laughed. "I didn't hear you come out here."

Liliana giggled and reached for her brother.

Manny picked her up. "I know we've forgiven; but if she does anything to make you feel bad, Bella, I will hit her."

Mama grabbed Manny's arm and pulled him down next to her on the bench. "I know you mean well, Manny, and want to protect your sisters, but we can't live like that."

"But remember, Papa punched that bad man. Two men. Tía Luisa is still pretty bad in my mind."

Mama smiled. "All right, if she tries to drag your sister off someplace, you go ahead and punch."

Bella grinned. "I can just see that. She grabs my arm and starts to run."

Manny handed Liliana back to his mother, then stood and started punching the air. "And if she does, I'll get her." They all laughed until their sides hurt.

After a few minutes, Mama stood and kissed both their heads. "Seriously, my loves, we are going to choose the higher way. We will be kind. We won't return hurt for hurt. We are going to live free."

"Okay," Bella and Manny chimed together. When Mama turned, the siblings rolled their eyes and high-fived each other.

"You two are funny, but I mean it."

Bella grabbed Manny's hand. "We know, Mama. And if Gabi could forgive what she went through, so can we."

Gabi joined them. "I have forgiven. But occasionally, I have bad dreams, or someone says something that makes me remember all the hurt and fear. But then, I make myself look at all that God has done in giving me you for a family. It helps me be thankful, not angry or scared. But if my dad or that bad man came here, it might be really hard."

Manny grinned. "I could punch them for you."

Gabi playfully punched his arm. "I'm so glad you're my brother, Manny. I think we'll be okay. What did the pastor say? With God, we can face fear and tell it to go away. We can do that if we help each other."

Bella stood and embraced her sister and sighed deeply. "I think we'll all be better than okay."

CHAPTER SIXTEEN

MAY, 1989

Sofia pulled the pan of cookies out of the oven as Manny burst into the kitchen and slammed the door behind him.

"Son, must you always slam that door? I almost dropped this pan, you startled me so."

"Sorry, Mama." He kissed her cheek. "But you need to hear this. A police officer just stopped me."

Sofia's face fell. "No. What happened? You haven't been in trouble for such a long time."

Manny shook his head and chuckled. "Oh, Mama. It's not trouble. He wanted to thank me."

Sofia rolled her eyes. "You sure about that? Tell me the truth, Manny." She set the hot pan on a towel on the table and placed her hands on her hips.

Liliana ran into the kitchen. "Mama, do you have any cookies?"

Sofia bent and kissed her cheek. "Right in that pan that I almost dropped." She looked askance at Manny, who just grinned. "Be careful. They're still hot."

"Thanks, Mama." She grabbed two cookies, blew on them to cool them, and scurried into the living room.

Turning to Manny, Sofia raised her eyebrows.

"Okay, two things, Mama. First, I approached this particular officer the other day and told him about a man I saw around Lili's school when I went by to walk her home."

Sofia's hand flew to her face. "Was he after our Lili?"

"He just hung around like he was waiting for his own child, but I stayed around a bit pretending Lili had forgotten something, and then he left. I saw him again the next day, so I told the officer that he just looked suspicious to me. I also told him how our family was involved in rescues and connecting kids to counseling."

Sofia put her hands on the sides of his face. "Such a good boy you've become."

"Awww, Ma. Let me finish. He started watching the guy and . . ." Manny lowered his voice, glancing into the living room. "He tried to grab one of her classmates. Thankfully, the policeman was right there and intervened. The guy is in jail. What's more, the second thing is that he asked if I'd talk to the elementary kids in Lili's school about staying safe. He's already cleared it with the administration. Next week."

"Manny, I'm so proud of you. Do you want one of your sisters to join you?"

"Bella and Gabi are already talking to the high school kids, and I think they're going to have an assembly with the middle school students."

Lili popped around the corner. "I listened to the whole thing. I know the girl, and she and I just talked about making posters to warn all the kids. We can make some about your talk or a list of things kids should pay attention to outside of school. Mama, you could help with that list, right?"

Manny grabbed a cookie and munched while Lili spouted all her plans. "Great idea, little sis. See if your friend wants to share her story, and you can make all the posters you want."

Sofia laid her hand on Lili's shoulder. "Make sure you talk to your friend's parents, and they give permission for her to tell what happened. And, of course, I will help. So will your papa."

That evening, the whole family sat down around the kitchen table to make plans and posters to assist kids and parents in remaining safe from those who would do evil. Bella and Gabi gave Manny pointers on how to present to the elementary children, and Sofia and Hector helped Lili form a list of pointers as well as resources for counseling.

Hector grinned. "We've come a long way, family. God has really been good to us. Let's always make plans to help others and always keep our eyes open and aware of danger."

CHAPTER SEVENTEEN

CHRISTMAS EVE, 2010

Hector chuckled at the commotion filling his home. Sofia scooped up one of the grandchildren and handed the toddler into his arms.

A siren sounded outside.

Sofia jumped and grimaced. "I guess Manny is off work. The neighbors will think we're making too much noise or worse when they see his squad car in the driveway."

A loud knock sounded at the door. Sofia shook her head and opened the door.

"Ma'am, do you have authorization to have this many people in the house? I've gotten several reports of too many cars on the street and loud noises." The officer stared her down.

"Manny, get in here before the neighbors start taking pictures. They're already starting to think we're drug dealers since 'the police' always arrive." She wrapped her arms around him and pulled him through the door. "Our wild little boy is now a grown-up police officer. It still amazes me."

Manny grinned. "My past sure gives me insight, Mama. Wild boys don't pull too many tricks on me. I know how they think."

"Son, you said you had an announcement, one that might not be that happy for us. Tell me before everyone descends into kissing you hello." Sofia looped her arm in his and entered the side room.

Manny placed his hand on his mother's cheek. "The higher-ups learned my background and yours and decided I should do a stint down at the border. I understand the experience and have compassion, and I know the laws. It's so different than when we came—it's incredibly more dangerous. They want me to share our story with the other officers."

Sofia leaned her head against his chest. "Oh, my boy. You are the best. You're strong. It was easier when your papa and I went into harm's way, but I know God will be with you. I will miss you. I will worry, but I will pray."

Manny lifted her chin and kissed her forehead. "I depend on your prayers, Mama. I think it will only be a couple months, and I'll certainly trust the Lord."

Little arms wrapped around Manny's legs and squeals filled the room. Several voices sounded. "Tío Manny is here!"

Soon, everyone crowded in the room, hugging and kissing.

Isobel called from the kitchen. "Little brother, get in here." Manny pulled away from his nieces and nephews, some of them chasing him into the kitchen. He embraced his sister. She glanced at her mother's face. "The news. You've told Mama. Give it up."

Gabi joined them, her little one in her arms, as Manny shared his announcement. A tear tracked down her face. "Oh, Manny, be careful. What will we do without you?"

"It won't be long. And this is Christmas Eve, a time to be happy." He turned and swooped up two of his nieces and twirled them around. They squealed and cried for more. As soon as he set the girls down, his nephews pulled him to the floor to wrestle.

Soon, Liliana called the boys to the table. "Time to eat."

Manny scrambled up off the floor and hugged her. "Lili, are you enjoying your school year?"

She sighed. "It's tiring, but I love teaching. I have two girls and a boy in my class who were trafficked. I really thank God every day for the church counselors. They've helped immensely, and the school has recommended them to so many families. There are just too many troubled kids—as Gabi knows all too well."

Gabi nodded while putting a bib on her youngest. "I'm only counseling part-time now, since this little guy arrived. You'd never know Manny isn't a blood brother. Everyone says this boy is just like him—busy and wild and tough. Not to mention, stubborn."

"Ha." Manny kissed her cheek and fist-pumped the eighteen-month-old. "Gotta be tough." His voice turned serious. "Gabi, have you done that new way of talking on the computer, even having more than one person, like a meeting with people all at different locations?"

"I have. I'm required to do some counseling that way when it's difficult for some people to come to my office or there's a need late at night. Why?"

Manny sat down and waited for Hector to pray for the meal. Sofia set a plate heaping with meat and rice and vegetables in front of him. He took a bite. "Gracias, Mama. Your food is the best." He glanced at Isobel and winked. "Your food, too, Bella." He took a sip of soda. "Well, Gabi, because of your own experience and your training as a counselor, I did tell the officials at the border about you when they interviewed me. They'd like to know if they can call on you, especially to counsel some of the kids."

"You know they can. And even though Mama doesn't have the license, she has the heart and know-how to lead them to the forgiveness and comfort they need. They could contact you, too, Mama, don't you think?"

Sofia wiped a tear sliding down her cheek. "I pray every day as I hear it's getting worse and worse. They can call me anytime."

Gabi wiped her son's face. "Manny, be sure to tell them that Mama and Papa trained so many how to recognize the signs of trafficking and set up networks with several hotels.

Manny nodded. "I did—and how they connected the hotels with law enforcement and churches that counsel."

Lili passed the meat to her husband. "What I love is the training they've provided to the schools, as well as the resources they need to rescue kids and to prevent it before it happens. I've used it in the classroom and in parent meetings."

Hector patted his wife's hand. "I'm available, too, anytime." His eyes twinkled. "Except when I'm having teatime with my granddaughters or playing soccer with my grandsons."

The oldest grandson smiled and talked with his mouthful. "I let Abuelito beat me today."

Manny slapped the table. "Be careful, those are fighting words. Your abuelito is pretty tough."

Hector laughed. "It won't be long before he'll be beating me, but don't tell him."

One of the granddaughters scrunched her face. "But, Abuelito, you just told him."

Hector bent toward her with his finger over his mouth. "Shhh."

Everyone laughed.

Isobel placed the last of the food on the table and sat across from Manny. "It's so good to see you. We will miss you so much. I've never gone that long without you around."

"I know. But it will go fast. And I told them about you, too. You've put so many of these sleazebags behind bars, and they're expanding the number of lawyers down there. None have the experience that you have. They even asked if you could come along."

Bella groaned. "Oh my, I don't think so. Gabi can show me how to do those computer meetings. I can always give advice."

Her husband, Nicolas, guffawed. "Yes, she will always give advice."

Bella made a face, and her kids giggled. "I know. I know. But it's because I'm so smart."

Conversations continued as they ate. Soon, all the children were playing and begging to open presents.

Sofia told them five minutes, and the older ones started a countdown. She sat next to her children and their spouses. "I just got word that Luisa's husband died. He was brother to your birth dad, Bella and Manny. I know we've had little contact with them since they came, but perhaps we need to attend the funeral next week."

Nicolas spoke first. "Bella, I know it was so hard, but it's been over twenty-five years. I think we should go."

Bella nodded. "We certainly should. I haven't sought out her or the cousins. And they haven't tried to see us. But it's time. Victor was always decent to us; but regardless, we walk in forgiveness now. Manny?"

"Absolutely." He grinned. "But I'm telling you, if she tries to drag you away, I will punch her—or, at least, put cuffs on her."

They all shook their heads and groaned.

Bella grinned. "Be sure to wear your police uniform, brother."

Gabi stood as her youngest headed toward the Christmas tree. "Aaron and I will be there."

Liliana stood. "Joel and I will also be there. But if you want a happy home here, we'd better get to opening the presents. The niños and niñas are restless."

Soon, paper and laughter were everywhere. Dads were putting in batteries, and mamas were oohing and aahing over all the wonderful presents.

Hector placed his arm around Sofia and whispered in her ear, "Look what God has done."

THE END

RESOURCES

For those who have been trafficked or are in danger of being trafficked
For those who suspect someone is being trafficked
For troubled young people
For those who would like to donate or volunteer

NATIONAL HUMAN TRAFFICKING HOTLINE

888-373-7888

Text INFO to 233733

www.Humantraffickinghotline.org

TIM TEBOW FOUNDATION

For info on anti-human trafficking and child exploitation, to join the
rescue team as an advocate or to pray, to donate financially, to volunteer

www.timtebowfoundation.org

NATIONAL CENTER FOR MISSING AND EXPLOITED CHILDREN

800-843-5678

www.missingkids.org (cyber tipline)

missingkids.org/gethelpnow/support/teamhope

COURAGEOUS AND FREE
Serenity Orchards, a place for girls who are survivors of
sex trafficking and abuse
1-833-ONEHOPE
www.courageousandfree.org

LOVE146
Journeys alongside children impacted by trafficking today and helps
prevent trafficking of children tomorrow
203-772-4420
www.love146.org

HOPE FOR THE CHILDREN MINISTRIES
Changing the Lives of Children and Families through Faith, Hope,
and Love
Working with At Risk, Under Privileged, Foster kids ages 11-18
727-459-5055
www.hftcm.org

READY FOR LIFE PINELLAS
Supports former foster care youth in homelessness prevention,
education, employment, and lifeline support
727-954-3989
www.readyforlifepinellas.org

SAK SUAM

A ministry dedicated to the prevention, rescue, restoration, transformation, and rehabilitation of vulnerable and exploited women, men, and children through vocational training and community development

www.saksaum.com

WOMEN AT RISK, INTERNATIONAL

Provides protection for the wounded, voices for the silenced, dignity for the abused, hope for women and children worldwide

(616) 855-0796

Tollfree: (877) END-SLAVERY

www.warinternational.org

WISCONSIN CHILD SEX TRAFFICKING AND EXPLOITATION INDICATOR AND RESPONSE GUIDE

dcf.wisconsin.gov

NATIONAL CHILD TRAUMATIC STRESS NETWORK

University of California: (310) 235-2633

Duke University: (919) 682-1552

nctsn.org/resources/all-nctsn-resources

5 STONES / FOX VALLEY
Three short films about the realities of sex trafficking
www.facebook.com/5stonesFoxValley

HOPE FOR JUSTICE
Non-profit organization that aims to end human trafficking
and modern slavery in the U.K., U.S., Cambodia, Norway, Australia,
Ethiopia, Uganda
www.hopeforjustice.org

ABOUT THE AUTHOR

J udy DuCharme grew up with Lake Huron next to her backyard. She, her husband, daughter, and son moved to Door County, Wisconsin, in 1984. After teaching fifth grade for twenty-two years, Judy followed the calling that had tugged at her all her life to write. *Who Will Rescue Us? A Love Story* is her tenth published book, and she is the recipient of numerous awards.

If you visit Door County, you may find her hiking in the woods, walking on the beach, jet skiing on the bay, e-biking with her husband, worshipping at her church, teaching a Bible study, cheering for the Green Bay Packers, playing with her grandson, or sitting outside enjoying the beauty around her.

Find out more about Judy at her website www.judithducharme. com or www.facebook.com/judy.ducharme.18 or www.instagram/ author_jducharme

Ambassador International's mission is to magnify the Lord Jesus Christ and promote His Gospel through the written word.

We believe through the publication of Christian literature, Jesus Christ and His Word will be exalted, believers will be strengthened in their walk with Him, and the lost will be directed to Jesus Christ as the only way of salvation.

For more information about
AMBASSADOR INTERNATIONAL
please visit:

www.ambassador-international.com

Thank you for reading this book!

*You make it possible for us to fulfill our mission,
and we are grateful for your partnership.*

*To help further our mission, please consider leaving us a review on your social media,
favorite retailer's website, Goodreads or Bookbub, or our website.*

MORE FROM AMBASSADOR INTERNATIONAL...

After his rescue from guerillas in Venezuela, Gideon finds himself with super-abilities, result from genetic engineering during his capture. When he returns home, he finds his beloved city in shambles and torn apart by crime. The police are understaffed and most do not care about the poor side, The Brooks. Gideon becomes a vigilante to protect his city and uses his newfound abilities. But he learns that being a vigilante comes with a price.

Betty is sure that Ida Lou does not belong in their church when the woman shows up to the Good Friday service with her small dog in tow. But before she knows what's happening, Betty— along with the other women of the WUFHs (Women United For Him)—is pushed into helping the woman. God works in mysterious ways—and through ordinary people. The town of Prosper is about to experience some drama—and it all starts with a dog who comes to church.

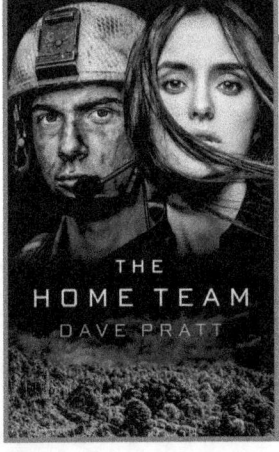

Sam Anthem has always been a team player, leading his Home Team on secret missions around the world. When he is forced on a vacation, he is introduced to a former covert ops soldier-turned pastor. But the vacation takes a turn when the Home Team comes under attack. As the team fights to stay alive against an unknown adversary, Sam begins to wonder if there is more to life than just the job. With his life on the line, Sam must decide between the job or his newfound faith and possible love.